KT-557-152

BOOK ONE: THE CONTEST

# EVEREST

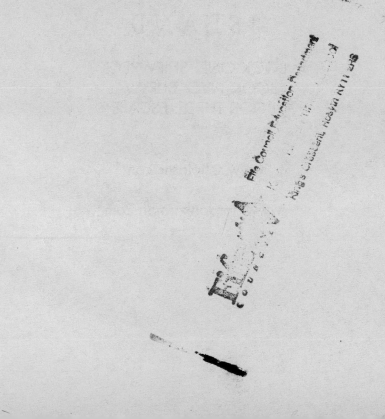

**A world of adventure from
Gordon Korman**

# EVEREST

## BOOK ONE: THE CONTEST
## BOOK TWO: THE CLIMB
## BOOK THREE: THE SUMMIT

# ISLAND

## BOOK ONE: SHIPWRECK
## BOOK TWO: SURVIVAL
## BOOK THREE: ESCAPE

www.scholastic.com

www.gordonkorman.com

# GORDON KORMAN

## BOOK ONE: THE CONTEST

# EVEREST

AN
**APPLE**
PAPERBACK

SCHOLASTIC INC.
New York  Toronto  London  Auckland  Sydney
Mexico City  New Delhi  Hong Kong  Buenos Aires

*For Brandon VanOver*

If you purchased this book without a cover, you should be aware that this book is stolen property. It was reported as "unsold and destroyed" to the publisher, and neither the author nor the publisher has received any payment for this "stripped book."

No part of this publication may be reproduced in whole or in part, or stored in a retrieval system, or transmitted in any form or by any means, electronic, mechanical, photocopying, recording, or otherwise, without written permission of the publisher. For information regarding permission, write to Scholastic Inc., Permissions Department, 557 Broadway, New York, NY 10012.

ISBN 0-439-40139-9

Copyright © 2002 by Gordon Korman.
All rights reserved. Published by Scholastic Inc.
SCHOLASTIC and associated logos are trademarks and/or registered trademarks of Scholastic Inc.

12 11 10 9 8 7 6 5 4 3 2 1       2 3 4 5 6 7/0

Printed in the U.S.A.                                        40

First Scholastic printing, August 2002

# PROLOGUE

It was a funeral in every way but one: The body was missing.

Not *missing*, exactly. Its location was common knowledge — that was the most horrifying part of all this. The body was nine thousand miles away in a country called Nepal, twenty-seven thousand feet up Mount Everest, the highest point on planet Earth.

On Everest, everything above twenty-five thousand feet is known as the Death Zone. There, overpowering wind gusts approaching two hundred miles per hour can wrench a strong person clear off the mountain, and bone-chilling nighttime cold of one hundred degrees below zero causes frostbite and hypothermia. Wherever the body was, it was surely frozen solid.

Twenty-seven thousand feet is above the range of any helicopter. At that altitude, the air is simply too thin to provide the rotor blades with any lift. A stranded climber would have a better chance of being picked up off the surface of the moon than in the Death Zone. Atop Everest, you

THE CONTEST

are your only rescue squad — you and the others who take on the mountain with you.

It was easy to spot those teammates among the mourners, and not just because of their young age. Their physical bodies fidgeted in the chapel, constricted by grief and tight collars. But their minds were still on the other side of the globe, five miles straight up, in the Death Zone.

They had that much in common with their unfortunate friend. It was a place they might never truly leave.

# CHAPTER ONE

Dominic Alexis arranged the caps and wrappers on his bedroom carpet and examined them for at least the hundredth time:

E EREST

He rummaged through the shoebox, searching for the V he knew was not there. R's. T's. Dozens of E's. He had counted once — more than fifty, and that was weeks ago. Even a few extra S's. Not a single V.

That was how these contests worked. Millions of the other letters were stuck under the caps of Summit Athletic Fuel and on the inside wrappers of Summit Energy Bars, distributed to stores all around the country. Then they printed up a grand total of three V's and shipped them to nonexistent addresses in Antarctica, fourth class.

He was exaggerating, of course. There were V's out there, even if just a handful. Over the past weeks, the TV news had shown clips of ecstatic young climbers who had spelled out EVEREST to qualify for the five wild-card spots at boot camp.

THE CONTEST

Four of those places had been filled. Only one chance remained.

At boot camp, the five lucky winners would join the American Junior Alpine Association's fifteen top young mountaineers for four weeks of intensive training and competition. It promised to be a brutal month of six-hour workouts, night climbs, and marathon hikes carrying heavy packs. But the end result was worth it. The top four climbers would earn places on SummitQuest — Summit Athletic's Everest expedition, the youngest team ever to attempt the world's tallest peak.

A shout from downstairs interrupted his reverie. *"Where's my sand?!"*

It was Christian, Dominic's older brother. Chris didn't have to scramble around garbage cans and recycling bins, scrounging for caps and wrappers. His place at boot camp was already secure. He was the number-two-rated under-seventeen climber in the country — second only to the Z-man himself, Ethan Zaph.

Chris was talking about his good-luck piece — a small glass vial of sand from the Dead Sea. It had been a gift from their grandmother, brought back from a trip to Israel when Chris was a baby and Dominic hadn't even been born. Chris loved the idea that the sand was from the lowest point on the globe. When he started climbing, he strung the vial on a leather cord so he could wear it around his neck. "I'm taking this sucker *vertical!*" he would say before an ascent. And at the top of the rock, or cliff, or mountain, he would talk to it: "Far from home, baby! You're far from home!"

It was natural that, as Chris became more accomplished as a climber, it would one day cross his mind to take his good-luck piece from the bottom of the world to the top of the world at the summit of Everest. Now, finally, he was getting his chance.

Pounding on the stairs. "Come on, Dom! I'm packing up my stuff for boot camp!"

There was no question that, right then, Dominic needed luck more than Chris did. The vial of sand clutched in his fist, he opened the sash of the window and expertly eased himself outside.

In many neighborhoods, it would probably raise eyebrows to have a thirteen-year-old climbing out a second-story window, but it was a fairly ordinary occurrence around the Alexis home. Sometimes it was just the easiest way down. Vertical was a forbidden direction for most people; for Chris and Dominic, it was as simple an option as left or right. Years before, as little kids, Chris had become the town hide-and-seek champion by scaling a fifty-foot tree for aerial surveillance every time he was "it." Even Mr. Alexis, when he needed to go up on the roof to check a flapping shingle, never bothered with a ladder. He had grown up in Switzerland, in the shadow of the high Alps, and was responsible for introducing his two sons to "this climbing foolishness." (Their mother's opinion.)

And anyway, a thirty-second climb was better than a face-to-face with Chris over a stolen — ahem — *borrowed* good-luck charm.

As far as degree of difficulty went, the front of the house was pretty pathetic. Dominic started down, jamming the edges of his sneakers into the narrow spaces between the bricks.

As he passed the picture window in the living room, he caught an exasperated look from his mother. He couldn't actually hear her, but instead read her lips as he dropped to the flower bed:

"We have a door . . ."

But Dominic was already sprinting along Mackenzie Avenue. Preparing for an ascent of Everest required workouts in the five- to seven-hour range, and he had been matching Chris step for step, pedal for pedal, and stroke for stroke. Only when climbing did Chris still hold an advantage. He was almost sixteen, bigger, taller, and stronger than Dominic. He could haul himself up a top rope as naturally as a yo-yo returns to the hand playing with it. Dominic was just a month past his thirteenth birthday, and small for his age.

The Mackenzie Avenue 7-Eleven was his home away from home. Dominic estimated he had drunk more than forty gallons of Summit Athletic Fuel in the process of spelling E EREST. He'd tried his share of the bars, too, but Summit Energy Bars were like quick-drying cement. After a few of them, your insides turned to concrete. Better to stick with the liquid.

*One more bottle. One last try.*

Out of habit, he checked the recycling bin behind the store first, but it was empty except for a couple of soda cans. Inside, he grabbed a bottle of Fruit Medley. The flavors didn't matter with Summit Athletic Fuel; it all tasted the same — like weak, slightly salted lemonade backwash. He paid, walked out, and flopped down on the wooden bench next to the store.

Before popping the cap, he addressed the good-luck charm the way he'd seen his brother do it. "Find me a V and it's Everest or bust! I'll take you to the top of the world!"

Sheepishly, he looked around to make sure no one had overheard. When Chris talked to his little vial of sand, it always seemed cool. But in the

7-Eleven parking lot, it was just plain embarrassing.

He twisted the cap off and peeked underneath.

Another E.

Until the wave of disappointment washed over him, he hadn't realized how much faith he'd had that his brother's good-luck charm would deliver.

The leather strap slipped from his fingers, and the vial dropped to the pavement and began to bounce down the small strip mall's parking ramp. Horrified, Dominic stumbled after it. Losing a shot at Everest was nothing compared with what he'd have to face if he came home without Chris's Dead Sea sand.

He scrambled like a crab, but the bottle rolled ahead of him, just out of reach. As he ran across the garage entrance, a hulking SUV roared up suddenly. The driver slammed on the brakes, and the big vehicle squealed to a halt just inches from the boy.

"What's the matter with you, kid? Why don't you look where you're going?"

"Sorry." Dominic picked up the vial and scooted out of the way. Mom had continuous nightmares that climbing would kill at least one member of her family. *I'll bet she wasn't expect-*

*ing it to happen like this,* he reflected, a little shaken.

The SUV accelerated up the ramp, pausing at the top. The driver tossed a candy bar wrapper into the trash barrel and drove off.

It was a Summit Energy Bar. Dominic recognized the logo from where he stood, rooted to the spot. He had climbed towering cliffs, yet walking up this gentle slope to get that piece of paper seemed much, much harder.

He reached into the garbage and fished out the sticky wrapper. In a way, he almost knew what he would see before he turned it over.

A V!

It was a ticket to the top of the world.

THE CONTEST

# CHAPTER TWO

Cap Cicero wasn't much of a worrier.

That time climbing Mount McKinley, when the boulder dropped from fifteen thousand feet and whizzed by so close that the wind almost knocked him off the fixed ropes, he didn't worry. His philosophy was, if it misses you, it didn't happen. And if it hits you, then you've *really* got nothing to worry about.

A worrier in the mountaineering business was like a surgeon who fainted at the sight of blood. Neither was likely to make it very far, and Cicero had been racking up death-defying feats and glorious triumphs for thirty-one of his forty-seven years.

But now, watching the twenty SummitQuest candidates, Cicero fretted that signing on as the team leader might have been a mistake.

"They're *children*," he told Tony Devlin, who ran Summit's Sports Training Facility in High Falls, Colorado. "A trip up Everest takes twenty-five pounds or more off the average adult. Half of these kids would fade to nothing."

EVEREST

"Relax," Devlin soothed. "Look at Ethan Zaph —"

"I know all about Ethan Zaph," Cicero interrupted. Several months before, Ethan had achieved fame by climbing Everest a few weeks shy of his sixteenth birthday — the youngest person ever to stand on top of the world. "So where is he?"

Devlin chuckled. "He knows he's got a spot guaranteed. Why should he suffer through a month of boot camp?"

Cicero harrumphed, but he knew Ethan Zaph wasn't the problem. At six foot one and 220 pounds, the kid was built like a lumberjack. Christian Alexis was also adult-sized. But Chris had brought his thirteen-year-old brother with him. Thirteen!

"That was a mistake," Cicero told Devlin. "Chris I understand. But the brother? Look at him. I don't think he's five feet tall."

Devlin shrugged. "We didn't pick him. He qualified as a wild card through the retail contest."

Cicero raised an eyebrow. "Lucky kid. Either that or he really likes Summit bars."

"Or maybe he just doesn't give up until he gets what he's after," suggested Devlin. "Not a

THE CONTEST

bad guy to have on an expedition. I hear he's an A-1 climber."

Cicero shook his head. "Too small. Can't use him."

"Do me a favor," said Devlin. "Don't cut him just yet. Summit got a lot of publicity out of that contest. We want to make it look like the wild cards have a real shot at the team."

Cicero nodded wisely. "And *then* we cut them."

"Not necessarily." Devlin reached out and pulled aside a sturdy runner with a mass of dark curls. "Here's one of our wild cards. Rob Barzini, meet Cap Cicero."

The boy turned shining eyes on the team leader. "It's an honor to meet you, Cap. I've read up on some of your expeditions." He grinned broadly, revealing an upper and lower set of gleaming braces.

Cicero regarded him in dismay. "When can you lose the iron?"

"The orthodontist says I've got another two years to go."

Cicero sighed. "Pack your bags, kid. I can't take that mouth into hundred-below windchill. The cold will bust your braces, and you'll be running around the Death Zone with a faceful of razor blades."

There were a few tears, but Rob accepted his fate and headed off to the office to arrange for an early flight home.

"You're a tough man," accused Devlin.

"It's a tough mountain." Cicero blew his whistle. All around the quarter-mile track, the candidates stopped running and turned to him for instructions. All except Dominic. He kept going, his twenty-pound pack whacking him between his narrow shoulders. The kid sure had stamina.

Cicero clapped his hands. "Okay, step it up! Double time. There's no dogging it on the mountain!"

The running resumed, faster this time. Dominic was practically sprinting now. The supreme effort only had the effect of making him look even smaller as he darted around the bigger kids.

One time, on K2, Cicero dropped his glove into a crevasse while securing a slipped ladder. He got stuck high on the Abruzzi ridge and had to bivouac — spend a forty-below-zero night in a cramped ice cave with his exposed hand jammed up the opposite sleeve clear to the armpit in order to prevent frostbite. He awoke to the agony of a dislocated shoulder, but he didn't panic.

Finding four climbers in this lot. *That* was a cause for panic.

THE CONTEST

*Okay*, he thought. Zaph and Chris Alexis. He needed only two more.

His eyes immediately traveled to Norman "Tilt" Crowley, who was lumbering steadily around the track. Tilt — great nickname for a climber — was younger than Ethan and Chris, but almost as big, with the same powerful build and easy athleticism. Plus, he was only fourteen. If Cicero could somehow get him to the top, it would smash Ethan's record by more than a year. SummitQuest would be on the front page of every newspaper on the planet — which was the whole idea. The purpose of this expedition was advertising, after all.

He watched as Tilt rounded the curve and came up behind Dominic. It happened so fast that the team leader wasn't really sure he had seen it. Tilt put his hands on Dominic's backpack and effortlessly leapfrogged over the smaller boy.

*Terrific*, Cicero groaned to himself. The last thing a high-altitude expedition needed was a hot dog.

His eyes shifted down the line. Sixteen-year-old Joey Tanuda was smaller and less impressive, but rock-solid, with a reputation as a great team player. Also, he had ice experience. Every winter, his parents took him to Alaska to climb frozen waterfalls.

He knew that Summit Athletic was also push-ing to put at least one girl on the team. Bryn Fiedler was the obvious choice. The country's top-rated female alpinist under seventeen, she was known to be a smart climber. Tall — five foot nine — and blessed with great arm strength, she was also tough. She had to be. Mountaineering was a sport dominated by men. Women climbers had to be bulldogs to get the respect they deserved, and Cicero figured the young ones had to try even harder than that.

Bryn aside, there weren't any girls who caught his eye, except —

The team leader stepped out into the track and plucked a Walkman and sunglasses off Samantha Moon, a fifteen-year-old brunette in a No Fear T-shirt. She was not only keeping pace with the other kids, but also windmilling air guitar as she ran. As the headphones cleared her ears, the pantomime power chords stopped, and so did Sammi.

She stared at Cicero in surprise. "What's up?"

"This isn't a fun run," he informed her hotly.

"Who said it was?" she retorted, snatching the headphones from his hands.

"People *die* climbing Everest," Cicero said. "I'll wash you out right now if you're not going to train seriously."

THE CONTEST

"I *am* training seriously," she shot back. "This" — more air guitar — "is just my style."

"Not on my expedition," he told her.

"Well, why didn't you *say* so?" She set the Walkman and glasses down at the side of the track and rejoined the running group, leaving Cicero shaking his head.

Devlin tossed him an offhand shrug. "If you don't like her attitude, cut her."

Cicero was tempted, but he held himself back. The truth was he didn't know a single top-notch alpinist who didn't have a bit of a screw loose. Aloud he said, "I'm keeping my options open."

Devlin pointed to a fifteen-year-old who sported the brightest orange hair Cicero had ever seen. "What do you think of the redheaded kid?"

"Easy to rescue," the expedition leader laughed mirthlessly. "We'll be able to spot him on the summit ridge all the way from base camp."

"Seriously," Devlin persisted.

Cicero followed the bouncing shock of hair. He was very much an "in the middle" teenager. Not tall, not short. Not fat, not thin. The kind of kid who'd get overlooked a lot — if it weren't for that lighthouse beacon on his head.

"Lazy," he observed, noting the lackluster

stride. "Not a good sign. But like I said, it's early. What's the big interest?"

"That's Perry Noonan," Devlin replied.

Cicero snapped to attention. "*The* Perry Noonan? He's here?"

"That's him," Devlin affirmed.

"Aw, Tony, we talked about this! I'm not doing anybody a favor putting a climber on that mountain who's not prepared."

Devlin met his gaze, and it was Cicero who looked away first.

"This is *my* decision," the team leader insisted. "That's in the contract. I'm the boss, right?"

"You're the boss of the expedition," Devlin agreed. "But there's always another boss. A higher boss, with the power to say something like, 'Maybe we won't climb Everest this year.' You know?"

Cicero thought back to the time on the north wall of the Eiger, when an ice screw snapped in two. He dropped sixty vertical feet and swung back into the rock face, shattering one ankle and spraining the other. He didn't panic back then. Who had the time? It would take all his skill and concentration to get down alive.

After what he'd seen and heard today, Cap Cicero was officially worried.

THE CONTEST

# CHAPTER THREE

The Summit Athletic Sports Training Facility in High Falls, Colorado, was nestled amid snow-capped peaks in the Rocky Mountains. Built on a plateau at eighty-five hundred feet above sea level, it was by far the highest such complex in the United States. At that, it was still nearly two vertical miles *lower* than Everest base camp, and more than four below the summit.

The facility had hosted some famous names from the world of sports — Tiger Woods, Michael Johnson, Kobe Bryant, Tony Hawk, and the entire U.S. Women's World Cup soccer team. But never had the place seen the kind of workouts that were going on as the nineteen remaining candidates fought to land spots on Cap Cicero's Summit-Quest team.

For three hours each morning, the class trained in the huge gymnasium. This included weight lifting, aerobic machines, calisthenics, and hours practicing rope techniques on the massive sixty-foot climbing wall built especially for this group. It was a grueling effort, but nothing compared with what was in store for the after-

EVEREST

noon. Cicero and his trainers would take them on six-hour hikes over some of the roughest and steepest terrain in North America.

"Cap, I gotta stop," gasped Cameron Mackie after nine miles under a thirty-pound pack. The trail they were following went up and down so often it had been dubbed the Toilet Seat. Climbers were notorious for nicknaming routes.

"What's the problem?" asked Cicero, barely breathing hard.

"The problem is we're dying back here," Tilt complained belligerently. "If we wrack ourselves up in boot camp, how are we supposed to climb Everest?"

Cicero nodded but never slackened the pace. "That's the rule for regular mountaineering. For high-altitude ascents in the Himalayas, you go till it hurts, and then work through it. You have to get used to carrying on when your body says quit."

Sammi looked out over a dizzying precipice. "Man, can you imagine hang gliding from here? What a rush!"

"A rush to the hospital," commented Bryn wryly. "Once they helicopter your broken carcass out of the trees."

"You'll never summit Big E watching your back like that," Sammi warned.

"I may not get to the top, but I guarantee I'll

make it back to the bottom," Bryn said seriously. "Climbing is about figuring the angles, predicting the hazards, and avoiding them."

"In some textbook," scoffed Sammi. "It's an extreme world out there. You've got to be extreme with it! My boyfriend and I tried bungee last week. Caleb liked it, but I say it's a little artificial. I mean, once you bottom out, you're just hanging there."

"And your folks let you do all this?" Bryn asked, amazed. Her own climbing career was a constant source of conflict between her mother and father. Not that Mom and Dad needed much help to fuel an argument.

She fought off a wave of guilt. They would have split up regardless of whether her hobby was climbing mountains or collecting stamps.

Sammi shrugged. "Dad thinks climbing E will calm me down. But what I really want to do is, there's this underwater cave off Australia where you can scuba with sleeping sharks."

Bryn had to laugh. "You never met a risk you didn't like, right?"

"Just one," said Sammi Moon. "Living a boring life."

Lenny Tkakzuk waved a video camera in their faces. He was the guide in charge of documenting the expedition for the SummitQuest Web site.

"Aw, come on!" Cameron rasped.

"You've all agreed to give interviews for the site," the cameraman/guide reminded him.

"You mean on E," said Sammi. "Who cares what we do in boot camp?"

"We think we can build up some interest in who's going to make the team. Let's see a little of that can-do attitude. Say something positive!"

"I'm positive I'm going to throw up," Cameron supplied.

Tkakzuk, Lenny's mind-boggling last name, was actually pronounced *ka-chook*, or, as he himself explained, "A sneeze between two k's." A few of the candidates started calling him Sneezy. Not only did the moniker stick, but it sparked a whole Seven Dwarfs nicknaming craze. The zombified kitchen manager became Sleepy. The Web designer, who never looked straight at anybody and whose best friends were probably all computers, was known as Bashful. Andrea Oberman, the expedition doctor, who was also a world-class climber, was Doc. No one was Dopey, or at least not yet. It was Dominic's opinion that the name was being held in reserve for whoever turned out to be dopey enough to claim it. Dominic felt that the smart money was on Tilt. Surely, the loudmouth was going to open his big yap one time too many and get himself bounced. Others insisted he was such a lock for Grumpy that to call him anything else was almost a crime.

Then there was Happy. He was a fifteen-year-old climber from California who always seemed to be in a good mood. According to Joey, his roommate, he smiled in his sleep. No matter how high Cicero twisted the agony meter on the afternoon marathon, Happy always seemed pretty thrilled about it.

"You think this is hard?" he'd say cheerfully. "This is nothing!" And he'd launch into a story of a killer rock climb in Yosemite.

Happy loved the cafeteria food. He thought the small dorm-style rooms they shared were the ultimate in luxury. Each night he spent hours in the computer lab, E-mailing his hordes of friends back home about how thrilled, excited, rapturous, and generally pumped he was.

"He's like a ray of sunshine," commented Joey. "I can't stand him."

That left Snow White. By unanimous agreement, the title was awarded to team leader Cap Cicero, because, as Sammi put it, "He's the unfairest of them all."

Cicero never seemed to run out of new and exciting ways to take the group through torture. When they got used to the thirty-pound packs, he made them carry forty. When they mastered the rough terrain, he found rougher. One time he led them on mountain bikes thirty miles to the top of a cliff called the Edge of the Earth. There, he had them descend on ropes with the bicycles strapped on their backs.

"You think this is hard?" beamed Happy. "At least it's cool. One time I got lost in the Pinnacles, and it was one hundred five degrees!"

When the indoor climbing drills became automatic, Cicero had a wrinkle to add to that, too. He led them through the same maneuvers lugging another climber, who was designated injured and unable to help.

"You can forget about me doing this on the real climb," Tilt grunted, struggling with Todd Messner's deadweight. "If one of you losers wipes out on Everest, consider yourself lucky if I don't step on your face on my way to the summit."

"And if *you* wipe out?" challenged Bryn, lowering Perry on a rope.

"It'll never happen," Tilt replied.

And watching his strength and confidence on the climbing wall, Bryn figured he was probably right.

That afternoon, five hours into a six-hour hike, Happy passed out cold halfway up a rock scramble called the Devil's Staircase. "You think this is hard?" he began, and then disappeared down the granite wedge.

Joey reached for his receding roommate, but overbalanced and fell. The unconscious Californian slid past Sammi and right between Tilt's legs. He was just about to drop off the slab when Bryn managed to trap him by pressing her backpack against the rock.

Luckily, Dr. Oberman was right there. After some water and a short break with his head between his knees, Happy was able to finish the workout.

The scare did nothing to wipe the perma-grin off his face.


*MEDICAL LOG — PSYCH PROFILES*
*Interview with Dominic Alexis*

**Dr. Oberman:** *How did you feel when Happy fainted today?*
**Dominic:** *I was sorry for him.*
**Dr. Oberman:** *Anything else?*
**Dominic:** *What do you mean?*
**Dr. Oberman:** *Fear, maybe? That it could happen to you?*
**Dominic:** *My dad has been training Chris and*

me. We know all the warning signs — dehydration, exhaustion —

**Dr. Oberman:** Some of the kids have been complaining that Cap is too hard on them.

**Dominic:** Cap Cicero is a legend! I've read all his books. I practically memorized his 1999 K2 expedition. I can't believe I got to meet him!

**Dr. Oberman:** Does it bother you that you're the youngest and the smallest?

**Dominic:** I'm used to it. I train with Chris all the time.

**Dr. Oberman:** Your brother has an excellent reputation. Is that why you were so obsessed with winning the contest? To keep up with him?

**Dominic:** I don't think I was obsessed.

**Dr. Oberman:** The contest people say you showed up with 145 drink caps and 36 energy bar wrappers. You had to know the chances were slim. What made you keep trying?

**Dominic:** I couldn't find a V.

Cicero looked up from the folder at Dr. Oberman. "What did you interview him for? I told you he's not going."

"I was curious about him," the doctor admitted. "He's such an intense little guy."

"And what did you find out?"

She grinned. "That he's honest, decent, dedi-

cated, motivated, healthy as a horse — exactly
the kind of person you'd want on an expedition."

"Yeah," Cicero snorted. "If he was a foot
taller, two years older, and forty pounds heavier."

She laughed. "You might also be interested to
know that he's a huge fan of yours."

"Good," said Cicero. "I'll give him an auto-
graphed copy of my memoirs. He'll need something to read while his brother is busy climbing
Mount Everest."

The next morning, Lenny "Sneezy" Tkakzuk got
up bright and early so he could film the Everest
hopefuls coming downstairs for breakfast. He
was the first to see the damage.

In the small lobby outside the cafeteria, someone had knocked over an end table, breaking
two of its legs and smashing a crystal lamp.

Ten minutes later, Cicero stood beside him,
wiping the sleep from bloodshot eyes. "You got
me up at six in the morning to show me a pile of
broken glass?"

Sneezy looked worried. "Think about our
kids, Cap. They're used to walking knife-edge
ridges over thousand-foot drops. They're not exactly the clumsy type."

"Don't talk to me in riddles. I'm not even

awake," complained Cicero. "Are you saying someone did this on purpose?"

"Either that or there was a big fight last night. We're driving these kids pretty hard, and there's a lot at stake here."

Cap sighed. "I could have taken those orthodontists up Nanga Parbat. But no. I had to play hall monitor to a gang of juvenile delinquents!" He ran his hand through his thick, uncombed hair. "All right. I'll talk to them."

THE CONTEST

# CHAPTER FOUR

It was a blinding blizzard, the kind that hit the Colorado mountains in January. The snow began just after dark, and by two A.M., when Cicero hauled the nineteen candidates out of their beds, there were already six inches of new powder on the ground.

"What's going on, Cap?" asked Chris, half asleep.

"Ever spend a night on the South Col of Everest?" Cicero asked.

"No."

"Well, this is the next best thing. Grab the tents. Camp-out tonight."

Bundled into their deep winter gear, they stumbled bleary-eyed into the storm. The biting cold woke them up in a hurry, but the operation of setting up aluminum poles was almost impossible in the blowing squall.

"Let's move," called Cicero. "You'll need to do this after eleven hours on the mountain." He turned to Sammi, who was flat on her back, napping, using the folded tent as a pillow. "What's

EVEREST

the matter, Moon? I thought you liked it extreme."

"Yeah, extreme snowboarding," came the groggy reply. "Not extreme snow."

The climbing brothers, Chris and Dominic, were used to working together. Theirs was the first shelter up.

"I said hold the flap, idiot!" Tilt roared at Perry.

"Okay, okay." The red-haired boy did his best to squeeze into what little space was left by Tilt's bulk.

"What a waste of time!" Tilt raged.

Cicero overheard him. "No, it isn't," he said seriously. "Where do you think you're going, summer camp? Training for hard work and miserable conditions is hard and miserable."

"So where's your tent?" challenged Tilt.

"I've already done this part of the training," Cicero replied.

"Easy for you to say," Tilt muttered under his breath.

"You want to see my diploma?"

Tilt glared back in defiance.

"Fine!" The expedition leader ripped off his left boot and then the sock. "Annapurna, 1989. My helmet lamp malfunctioned, and I had to spend a night at twenty-five thousand feet. The thing about frostbite is, there isn't any pain. You just feel numb. But it's worse than pain because you know what's happening to you."

The candidates gawked. The two smallest toes were missing from Cicero's foot. It was a cruel truth of high-altitude climbing. There was only one treatment for the worst kind of frostbite — amputation.

For the Everest hopefuls it was a reality check. They were all accomplished alpinists, but were they ready for the brutal toll that the great mountains could impose? Even Tilt was struck dumb.

"This is Honolulu compared with where we'll be in a couple of months," Cicero informed them harshly. "Aloha." It would have been an ideal moment to stride dramatically away. But since his boot was off, he had to hop, muttering under his breath as he disappeared into the storm.

"There goes one of the all-time legends," Dominic said admiringly.

"There goes one of the all-time crackpots," Tilt amended. "Like I need to look at his freak-show foot."

Chris glared at him. "You may be a good climber, Crowley. But it's going to take a long time before you've got the experience of that man."

Tilt spread his arms wide. "Forgive me for

thinking it's stupid to freeze out here for nothing."

"This is exactly the kind of camping we'll have to do on Everest," Dominic argued.

"And on Everest, I won't mind doing it!" Tilt roared. "But not when I've got a nice comfortable bed on the other side of that door!"

The tents offered protection from the wind and snow, but not the cold. The candidates snuggled deep in their sleeping bags and tried to stay warm. The space was so confined that they found themselves pressed together like sardines. It made sleep impossible.

"If you don't get your elbow out of my back, you're never leaving this tent alive," Tilt promised Perry.

"I can hardly move," Perry complained. He tried to get comfortable, but Tilt's bulk kept him pinned against the sidewall. "Hey —"

"What's the problem, rich boy? Accommodations not to your liking?"

Perry stared at him. "What are you talking about?"

"Look at your stuff. Titanium crampons. The best ice ax money can buy. Gore-Tex everything." He tweaked the fabric of Perry's jacket. "Heat panels, right? You're toasty warm while the rest of us freeze."

"It was a present —"

"You're loaded."

"My dad works at the post office," Perry insisted stubbornly.

"You mean he *owns* it."

Perry sighed. "I've got a rich uncle, okay? He's the one who pays for all my stuff."

"You should get him to buy you some talent," the big boy taunted. "You climb like my grandmother."

Perry wasn't even insulted. The fact was, he reflected unhappily, if it were possible to purchase mountaineering ability, Uncle Joe probably would have given him that, too, along with the lessons, and the equipment, and the clothes. Money was no object for Uncle Joe.

It was great and terrible at the same time.

And now it was starting to get out of control.

# CHAPTER FIVE

For Perry Noonan, having a billionaire uncle was a lot like playing Twister with an elephant. No matter how well-meaning the animal is, you can't help but get pushed around a lot. Joe Sullivan's own alpine dreams were replaced by high blood pressure and a business that took up twenty-five hours of every day. That was when the bachelor CEO had traded in his ice ax and high-altitude gear for weekend climbs with his only nephew in the foothills outside Boulder.

And Perry had said yes. Of course it was yes. What kid would turn down a chance to spend time with the family legend? A man who was constantly in the paper or on TV? Never mind that Perry might have preferred to go to a hockey game with his uncle, or even take him on in a spirited chess match. (Chess — that was something Perry was good at.) But this was Joe *Sullivan*. If he wanted to hang out with you, out was where you hung. And if that meant climbing, so be it.

Climbing — Perry shuddered. He could do it. He even got pretty good at it. But the unnaturalness of it — the feeling that he was where he

THE CONTEST

wasn't supposed to be — that never went away.

*If God wanted me to get up that rock face, he would have installed stairs.* It was an old joke, but Perry truly believed it. To him, there was something in a steep cliff or a rough crag that plainly said: *You don't belong here. Stay away.*

Over the years, he had learned to control the uneasiness. Something as simple as not looking down helped a lot. And the rope work kept his mind engaged. Belaying — the placement of bolts, anchors, and cams so that a climber can be secured by a companion in the event of a slip — took a lot of concentration. Because it kept his mind off of where he was and what he was doing, Perry had become a great belayer.

It made Uncle Joe proud. "I love watching you handle those ropes, kid. You're a natural!"

Uncle Joe never quite figured it out: Perry Noonan was good with ropes precisely because he *wasn't* a natural. He had been faking it all these years — up all those crags, all those gorges and cliffs. Now he was going to try to fake his way up the tallest mountain on Earth, twenty-nine thousand feet of not looking down. And just because he didn't have the guts to disappoint Uncle Joe.

His reverie popped like a bubble, and Perry was back in the tent.

He rolled over in the tight space. "It doesn't matter how I got here," he muttered in the darkness. "I'm not going to make the team anyway."

"You got that right," snorted Tilt.

It was Perry's one consolation. There was no way an expert like Cap Cicero could fail to notice that Perry didn't exactly measure up to his fellow candidates. For starters, Ethan Zaph would be coming soon. He was as good as 90 percent of the adult alpinists in the world and had summited Everest already. Then there were guys like Chris and Joey — *and* Tilt, who was a loudmouth and a bully, but athletically, a Mack truck. Even a couple of the girls seemed miles ahead of Perry. He thought of Bryn's confident efficiency and Sammi's fearlessness. This was more than a hobby to them. It was a way of life. Half the kids spent their free time bouldering. Nine hours of workouts a day, and these guys choked down lunch so they could race outside the complex and find a twenty-foot rock to scale. For *fun*.

Perry didn't belong on the same mountain with them. They were the kind of people who looked down.

He peered through the tent flap. All was quiet except for a shadowy figure about fifty feet away, barely visible in the storm. As he squinted

THE CONTEST

through the blowing snow, whoever it was tumbled over the rise and disappeared down the slope.

"Hey!" He grabbed Tilt's sleeping bag. "Somebody fell!"

"Not my problem," the big boy mumbled, turning over.

Perry burst out of the tent in a full sprint — or at least as much of a sprint as was possible plowing through snow. He peered down the hill. There was very little light, but he could hear distant screaming and could make out a dark shape plunging into the valley at unnatural speed.

He scrambled down the slope, breathing a silent prayer that he wasn't in hot pursuit of some kind of wolf, or worse, a bear. At the bottom, there was a shower of white and the figure disappeared. Perry rushed over.

"Hello?" he called. "Hello, are you all right?"

The snow shifted, and a frosted Sammi Moon sprang up, eyes shining. "Not bad!" She reached down into the drift and came up with a plastic garbage can lid. "I wonder if there's some way I could get this waxed."

Perry stared at her. "It's two-thirty in the morning! I thought you'd fallen over the edge!"

"I couldn't sleep," Sammi said innocently. She held out the lid. "Want to try?"

*Correction*, Perry reflected, amending his thought from before. He didn't belong on the same *planet* as these people.

The next morning, the camp awoke to clear blue skies gleaming off a foot of fresh snow. The storm was over. Dominic rushed to unzip the tent, eager for his first blast of warming sun. Instead, he found himself staring into the weathered face of Cap Cicero.

"All right, vacation's over!" the team leader bawled. "Everybody into the gym! We've got a mountain to get ready for!"

Tilt was belligerent. "I can't believe you made us do this!"

Cicero winced. "Change of plan, everybody. First mouthwash, *then* into the gym."

By the end of the day, two more SummitQuest candidates had quit and were on their way to the airport in Denver. Happy was one of them, smiling no longer. His parting words were: "It's too hard. It's the hardest thing I've ever done."

Perry had never even learned his real name.

THE CONTEST

# CHAPTER SIX

The first round of official cuts was scheduled for the end of that week. Everybody realized it was coming, but nobody knew exactly what to expect. Would Cicero pull you aside and give you the bad news? Or maybe Sneezy, or Dr. Oberman? Would it be public? Would you be yanked away from the dinner table and marched off in disgrace? Maybe it would be the opposite of that: You'd wake up in the morning, and a whole bunch of kids would be just plain gone. And, of course, the million-dollar question: Who?

One thing was certain. As the time approached, the tension rose so high that you could almost hear a hum throughout the complex.

Tilt thought he might be the most nervous of the lot. It was crazy. What did he have to worry about? He was the best climber in the group, except maybe for Ethan Zaph, who still hadn't shown up. But Tilt was worried about all the mouthing off he'd done to Cicero. Not that the dictator didn't deserve it. The guy was on some kind of power trip and got his jollies by bossing

EVEREST

around a bunch of kids. But maybe it was stupid to bug the person who was in charge of picking the team. Tilt would have only himself to blame if he washed out.

And he needed this more than the others. *Tilt Crowley, the youngest kid to climb Everest. Buy this breakfast cereal; it helped Tilt Crowley reach the top of the world. Oh, Harvard needs a man like Tilt Crowley.* How else was he going to get to the Ivy League? Was he supposed to pay the tuition by working himself to death on a triple paper route, the way he'd bought his secondhand crampons? And the ice ax with the slightly warped handle? The other kids here all had state-of-the-art stuff. That was Tilt's definition of rich people. He didn't mean mansions and private jets, like Perry's uncle probably had. Rich was anyone who could climb as a hobby — a hobby that wasn't attached to a second career, seven miles a day, lugging the *Cincinnati Inquirer* through sleet or hundred-degree heat. If he made it to the summit, only he would know that the mountain had been the easy part of the ascent.

Sure, he realized the others didn't like him. They climbed on ropes; he climbed on attitude. If he had their advantages, he could be a nice guy, too. Maybe he *should* have been nicer. Maybe he was going to be cut now for getting on people's nerves — on *Cicero's* nerves.

*Come on, Cap, don't wash me out! I'm the best you've got. And I need this!*

It finally happened after a thirty-mile hike with full gear through the snow. Seven lockers in the equipment room were tagged with yellow Post-it notes. *See Cap* was all they said. But everyone knew instantly. The ax had taken its first swing.

Four boys and three girls were headed home. Their Everest dreams were over.

Astonishingly, Joey Tanuda was one of them.

"But you've been eating Cap's workouts for lunch!" exclaimed Bryn.

Joey could only shake his head miserably.

Sammi was also surprised. "I mean, *Perry* made it, and you're twice the climber he is!"

"Hey!" Perry said feelingly.

"No offense, but it's true," Sammi persisted. "Why cut him and not you?"

Joey was so devastated that he could barely raise his gaze from the floor tiles. "A couple of years ago, I broke my nose bouldering, and the surgeon offered to do a nose job while he was in there anyway. I figured I might as well be beautiful, right? Now Andrea says my nasal passages are too tight for easy breathing when the air gets thin high on the mountain."

"Won't the bottled oxygen help?" asked Chris, feeling the other boy's pain.

"Not enough," said Joey. "I'm done."

"And after all that, you're still ugly," observed Tilt, kicking his climbing boots into his locker.

"I love you, too," Joey mumbled miserably.

Chris turned on Tilt. "The guy just washed out for something that's not even his fault. Think maybe now isn't the time for jokes?"

Tilt shrugged nonchalantly. "Who's joking?"

Joey glared at him. "You know what would make this okay? If you're next."

"Dream on, nose job," sneered Tilt. "I'm the best climber in this dump."

"Maybe so," said Joey. "But you're a self-centered jerk. There's no place for that on a climbing team." He shouldered his duffel and stood up.

"Sure, go ahead and hate me," invited Tilt. "But I'm the only honest one here. These guys all act like your best friends. But they don't want to admit that, deep down, they're celebrating. With you gone, one more spot on the team is up for grabs."

There was an awkward, embarrassed silence

as the truth of Tilt's words sunk in. Joey had been a favorite to make the chosen four. Sad as it was, his departure meant better chances for the remaining climbers.

"Hey," Joey said in a subdued tone. "I've got no hard feelings. I'll be following along on the Web site, pulling for you guys. Most of you," he added with a dirty look at Tilt.

Sneezy entered to record the parting on video. He was almost as disconsolate as Joey. "Sorry, kid. I know it's hard, but I've got to shoot this for the site."

Joey smiled halfheartedly. "Don't worry, Sneezy. We all knew the rules before we got here." With the camera running, he turned to Chris. "This is my Cub Scout mountaineering badge," he said, holding out a tattered piece of felt. "It's the first climbing thing I ever won. I want you to leave it on the summit for me."

Chris accepted the token. "If I get there, you get there," he promised.

And then there were ten Everest hopefuls left in the Summit Athletic Sports Training Facility.

What none of them knew was that, during the hike, Cap Cicero had actually affixed eight Post-it notes, not seven. The extra cut had been Dominic Alexis. Cicero had made the decision with regret.

The boy was a talented climber with incredible stamina and unfailing courage. But Cicero had felt from the start that the kid was too young and too small. So Dominic was out.

Later, Cicero was in Dr. Oberman's office, examining the candidates' chest X rays, which were all lined up across a wide viewing box. It was important for kids especially to have good lung capacity on Everest, where there was so little oxygen in the air.

He was looking with approval at an assortment of healthy chests when Tony Devlin ran up, all atwitter. "You have to change the cut."

Cicero looked surprised. "Why? Perry's still alive — not that you can tell from his effort level."

"This isn't about Perry," Devlin explained. "You've sent home all the wild-card kids."

Cicero adjusted the backlight. "Yeah, and I wonder why. Everest isn't a theme park, you know. You don't take tourists up there."

"The retail contest focused a huge amount of attention on SummitQuest," Devlin argued. "Already the newspapers and wire services are running updates from our Web site. It's like *Survivor*. People want to know who's going to make it. It looks bad if all the contest kids wash out by the first cut."

THE CONTEST

"It looks worse if we leave them dead in the Khumbu Icefall," Cicero said shortly.

"I'm not saying they have to end up on the team," Devlin reasoned. "Just keep one of them in the running a little longer so we can play it up on the site. Make it seem like the contest wasn't totally bogus — you know, like this kid really has a chance to go."

"It's not fair to the kid, either," Cicero noted. "These workouts aren't exactly patty-cake."

"Just do it," coaxed Devlin. "You of all people know how important it is to keep the sponsor happy."

It was true. Star alpinists would be stopped in their tracks if a disgruntled sponsor cut off the shipments of food and equipment.

"Fine." The team leader's eyes scanned the X rays and came to rest on the scrawny body that could belong only to one person. He blinked. Dominic Alexis was half the size of the others, but he had a chest full of dark, expanded lung tissue that would be the envy of anyone there. *He may be small,* Cicero reflected, *but he has the respiratory system of a six-foot-five bodybuilder.*

"We'll keep the little guy," he said suddenly. "Just till the next round. Then he's history."

"Thanks, Cap." A satisfied Devlin headed off to remove the Post-it from Dominic's locker.

## MEDICAL LOG — PSYCH PROFILES
### Interview with Perry Noonan

**Dr. Oberman:** You seem surprised that you survived the first cut.

**Perry:** No, I'm not. I'm as good as anybody here, right?

**Dr. Oberman:** What do you think?

**Perry:** I've been climbing since I was nine.

**Dr. Oberman:** With your uncle?

**Perry:** Right.

**Dr. Oberman:** Do you want to climb Mount Everest?

**Perry:** Every mountaineer —

**Dr. Oberman:** Not every mountaineer. You. Do you want to climb Everest?

**Perry:** Yes.

**Dr. Oberman:** You're sure about that?

**Perry:** What do you want me to tell you? That it's less than useless? That if you're going to spend zillions of dollars on something that's practically impossible, you might as well be curing cancer, or stopping wars, or feeding the hungry? Well, forget it. People climb mountains, period. And the biggest one is the one they want to climb most.

**Dr. Oberman:** And that includes you?

**Perry:** Yeah, sure. Why not?

THE CONTEST

**Dr. Oberman:** *I'm not hearing any straight answers.*
**Perry:** *I'm not hearing any straight questions.*

The kitchen manager, aka Sleepy, escorted Cicero around the wreckage of the crockery cabinet. The breakfront itself was tipped over on the floor. Around it were a million shards of broken glass and dishware.

The team leader was appalled. "My guys did this?"

"Unless we have a poltergeist," Sleepy said grimly.

Dr. Oberman spoke up. "I've been doing psych evaluations on all the kids. I could be wrong, but nobody jumps out at me as a vandal."

"Psych, my butt!" seethed Cicero. "It's Tilt Crowley! He's gone, first thing tomorrow morning."

The doctor was shocked. "You can't do that. You have absolutely no proof!"

"The Supreme Court needs proof!" Cicero raged. "I'm instant law! Ask any of the kids, and they'll tell you Tilt's the one."

"He has a lot of anger," Dr. Oberman agreed. "And there may be good reasons to send him home. But this isn't one of them. For starters, I don't think he did it. And if I'm right, the real culprit would still be here, and might even end up on the team."

"What about my dishes?" Sleepy demanded.

Cicero could only shake his head. "Charge them to the expedition, I guess." To the doctor he said, "I don't care about the money. It's the distraction that worries me. We can't lose our focus. Not on Everest. Not when we're facing the Death Zone."

THE CONTEST

# CHAPTER SEVEN

The cuts brought a change in the atmosphere at the Summit complex. When the Everest hopefuls had been twenty in number, the final team had seemed very remote. Now they were ten, vying for four spots. And even though the top place was being held for Ethan Zaph, the odds were improving. The candidates could almost feel their crampons biting into the blue ice of Everest's glaciers. The biggest prize in mountaineering was slowly coming within reach.

A new sport was born, one that was almost as popular as climbing: figuring the angles.

Cameron Mackie was an expert at it. "Z-man takes the number-one spot; Chris gets number two — that's pretty definite."

"And one of the girls," put in Dominic. There were three left.

"Bryn," mused Cameron. "Then again, you can't write off Sammi. She's crazy, but she's good."

Dominic did the math. "That leaves only one spot for the rest of us. Probably Tilt."

"Tilt's too dumb," Cameron said seriously.

"He'll give Cap a wedgie and get himself cut. So, depending on the Perry factor, if I keep my nose clean, maybe I can sneak in the back door."

*The Perry factor* was the question of why Perry was still standing after much stronger climbers had been packed off to the airport.

"Maybe Cap thinks I'm good," was Perry's explanation. "Maybe you guys are wrong about me." But he didn't sound convinced.

"Maybe Cap's your rich uncle," sneered Tilt.

Perry said nothing. He had often thought of having a different uncle, but in his imagination it was always a nonclimber who thought the Himalayas was a chain of doughnut shops.

"It's getting weird," Bryn admitted to Sneezy in an on-camera interview for the Web site. "Normally, climbers are the friendliest people on the planet. You take six total strangers scaling El Capitán, and by lunch you've got six best buddies. Here you want to be nice to people. But part of you says that, if they do well, it could cost you *your* chance."

Nowhere was that more true than with Bryn and Sammi. Both were convinced that only one female would advance to the final team. So their competition, they felt, was solely between them and the other girl, who wasn't really a threat. Their growing friendship cooled. They weren't en-

THE CONTEST

emies, but they became afraid to trust each other.

Tombstone IV was a black crag, not enormous, but steep and awkwardly shaped — the toughest piece of technical mountaineering the candidates had tackled so far. The route required them to get over a rocky spur called the Club, and while they were climbing up the underside, they would be hanging exposed over a hundred-foot drop.

"Extreme," breathed Sammi reverently.

"I'm really starting to hate that word," groaned Bryn.

Bryn inserted a spring-loaded CAM in a crack on the bottom of the spur and watched the unit expand to secure the protection point. Sammi passed a rope through the ring and then wiggled out to place a second piece of hardware. But as she tried to scramble around to the top, the tangle of lines imprisoned her ankle. Bryn climbed out and reached to free her partner's leg.

And froze.

High up the crag, the two girls' eyes locked, and the message passed between them as if by radar: *If I leave you here and go for help, Cap could cut you for a beginner's mistake and then I've got a guaranteed spot on the team.*

The moment was over as quickly as it had unfolded. Bryn broke out of her inaction and undid the snarl of rope around Sammi's ankle. The two clambered atop the Club and rested, eyeing each other suspiciously.

"Was that what I think it was?" panted Sammi.

And Bryn could only shrug miserably. Helping a fellow climber should be as automatic a response as a dog chasing a stick. What was this competition doing to them?

"This is so bogus," Sammi complained to Dominic that night. "No mountain is worth it."

"This one is," Dominic said simply. He couldn't help noticing that, as his fellow climbers became cagier with one another, they were growing more open with him. That meant no one, not even his own brother, felt he had a shot at making the team.

Dominic himself didn't really expect to last much longer.

The cold air of the Rockies was rife with competition. Six-hour workouts now took five. Everything was speeded up as the candidates competed for Cap Cicero's attention.

Even leisure time was turning into a tournament. Bouldering after lunch had become an ex-

THE CONTEST

tension of boot camp, despite the fact that Cicero and his guides weren't even watching. It was now a full-blown obsession.

Dominic scrambled up a twenty-foot rock, scanning for handholds the way a chess master seeks out weaknesses in an opponent's defenses. On the other side of the craggy diorite outcropping, Tilt raced against him with strong, steady moves. Dominic couldn't see his adversary, but he had a good idea of his progress because Tilt climbed with his mouth as much as he did with his hands and feet.

"Getting tired, shrimp? You can't beat me. If you're looking for the top, just follow the soles of my boots. . . ."

"Tilt Crowley," Perry said with a sigh, watching from below. "The only climber who uses trash talk."

In a mammoth burst of energy, Tilt scrambled to the crown of the boulder and stood there, beating his chest and howling like Tarzan.

From below, Dominic snaked out a hand and began to feel for a handhold on the top. Tilt stuck out his boot and applied gentle pressure to the searching fingers. "No way, shrimp. This is *my* rock."

Dominic gave no answer, but it was not in his nature to retreat.

The boot pushed a little harder.

"Geez, Tilt," coaxed Perry, looking up at the two, "leave him alone."

Tilt nodded. "As soon as he gives." The foot bore down.

Dominic gritted his teeth against the pain. Because of the angle of the rock, he couldn't see his tormentor. But he could picture Tilt's expression of nasty triumph. It made him more determined than ever to hang on.

Perry searched the group and spotted Chris. He caught the older boy's attention and redirected it with a nod to the standoff atop the boulder.

Chris loped over. "Come on, Tilt. Let him up."

"No chance," said Tilt. "My summit, my record."

"What are you talking about?" asked Perry. "Half the kids have been up that thing."

"I'm the youngest, and that's what counts," Tilt said stubbornly. "The shrimp's younger than me, so he's not going."

"Is that how it's going to be on Everest, too?" challenged Chris.

A derisive snort. "No one's taking this runt to Everest." Now Tilt was leaning on the fingers. Dominic saw stars.

Chris established one handhold and one

THE CONTEST

foothold. "If I have to come up there, your descent is going to be fast and headfirst!"

"You think?" Tilt snarled defiantly.

Todd Messner came running down the path, waving a copy of the *National Daily*. "Hey, guys! Check it out! We're in the paper!"

Tilt stepped off Dominic's hand. "You're lucky, shrimp. My public awaits." He climbed effortlessly down and joined the crowds around Todd.

The article was a double-page spread in the sports section under the headline:

### FROM DAY CAMP TO BASE CAMP

In a few weeks, the youngest expedition ever will set out for the world's highest mountain. But will their adolescent hang-ups prove to be a bigger obstacle than Everest?

"Hey, wait a minute —" began Chris in protest.

The article was very different from the kind of information Sneezy was posting on their Web site. It said almost nothing about the SummitQuest training or the upcoming climb. Instead, it was written like a reality-TV episode, focusing on personal habits, embarrassing details, and petty squabbles. And the general tone of it seemed to ask, *How can these kids form a team to survive the Death Zone when they can't even agree who gets to use the bathroom first?*

"Hey, that only happened once!" exclaimed Perry.

Chris's face was carved from stone. "There's no way they could know this stuff about us!"

Somehow, the *National Daily* reporter had found out that Bryn's parents were filing for divorce, and the argument over sending their daughter to Everest had been the final blow to a shaky marriage. It was also stated that Chris was on academic probation at school, and the expedition would probably cost him a year. The fact that Sammi was E-mailing her boyfriend back home was blown out of proportion. According to the article, every other sentence out of her mouth was "Caleb did this" or "Caleb said that." The gutsy, in-your-face athlete came across as a lovestruck ditz.

It went on: Cameron was in phone contact with his psychiatrist. Tilt was unpopular. Perry wasn't good enough. Dominic was too young and skinny. And Cap Cicero, famous alpinist and guide, was an inflexible bully who lived by the adage *My way or no way.*

"I don't get it!" exclaimed Todd. "I mean, it's all true, but — how did *they* find out?"

THE CONTEST

"Obviously," said Chris, "there's a rat around here. The question is who."

Tilt shrugged. "Simple. One of the guys who washed out got mad and squealed to the newspaper. It's no big deal."

"That's easy for you to say," put in Todd. "You're just unpopular. But Sammi's going to have a heart attack when she sees this."

"Not to mention Cap," added Perry.

"Cap's a big boy," put in Chris.

"Cap's a big jerk," Tilt amended. "But he's used to the media." Out of the corner of his eye, he spotted Dominic sitting cross-legged atop the mass of diorite. The younger boy's face radiated defiance.

"Your brother's spooky," Tilt informed Chris.

"Tell me something I don't know."

Bryn sprinted through the trees, all breathless excitement. "Sammi's found a monster problem down in the valley!"

In bouldering, a "problem" was a large, technically difficult rock. Climbing it was referred to as "solving."

They all raced after Bryn, including Dominic, who had to rush to catch up after descending the disputed boulder.

In a broad valley, almost hidden by a grove

of pines, stood the ultimate rock formation. It was three stories high and resembled a mammoth mushroom sitting atop a lopsided pedestal. As they watched, Sammi Moon scrambled up on the base and began to work her way onto the stem of the mushroom.

Perry waved. "Way to go, Sammi!"

"Shhh!" The others glared him into silence. No true climber would ever distract a fellow alpinist who was in the middle of taking on a tough problem.

Sammi reached the "ceiling" and clung there in the shadow of the enormous slab that made up the mushroom crown. It stretched at least seven feet around her in all directions. She reached up and ran her hand over the smooth limestone. She managed to get a finger lock in a small fissure and hung, twenty-five feet above them, searching for another hold. But there was nothing.

She paused for a moment, taking stock, then began to sway back and forth in an effort to swing her legs over the edge of the mushroom and find purchase on the top.

"Don't do it," urged Chris under his breath.

"Of course she'll do it," whispered Tilt. "Somebody get a mop."

But Sammi didn't like her chances and pulled

THE CONTEST

her lithe body back to the stem for a descent.

Tilt passed her on the way up. "Not very extreme," he commented cheerfully.

"You won't make it, either," she promised, tight-lipped.

She was right. First Tilt, then Bryn, then Todd were unable to get to the top of the mushroom. Chris, who was tallest, managed to get a foot over the edge of the crown, but couldn't find anything to latch onto up there and had to retreat. Dominic had the least success of all. His reach was too short to make it to the first finger lock, so he never got off the stem.

Cameron was smiling as he dipped his hands in the chalk bag. "Watch," he grinned, "and take notes." He had noticed a different hold, this one closer to the edge. The fissure was even narrower, but he succeeded in hooking two fingers into it.

There was no warning. A small shower of dust rained down at the same time the handhold crumbled.

# CHAPTER EIGHT

Legs windmilling wildly, Cameron dropped fifteen feet straight down and bounced off the pedestal. He hit the ground like a ton of bricks and lay there, unconscious.

Chris got to the fallen climber first. "Find Cap!" he barked at the others. He looked at the trickle of blood coming from the corner of Cameron's mouth. "And Andrea!"

Bryn, who was the fastest runner, took off for the complex.

Sammi stepped toward Cameron, but Dominic held her back. "We can't move him," he warned. "He could have a broken neck."

There was no panic. The candidates fidgeted in grim acceptance. In their sport, the thrills were many, but the mishaps were often deadly.

Todd removed his glasses and held them in front of Cameron's nose. The lenses fogged. "He's still breathing."

The roar of a motor shattered the mountain quiet. The SummitQuest candidates watched as an all-terrain vehicle plowed down into the valley in a shower of powdery snow. As it drew closer,

THE CONTEST

they could make out Cicero at the wheel. Beside him rode Dr. Oberman, with Sneezy and Bryn in the back.

The doctor leaped off the still-moving ATV and rushed to Cameron's side. Shedding her gloves, she lifted his eyelids and examined his pupils. Then she checked his pulse.

She addressed the nine candidates who were hovering around. "Don't look so tragic. He's not dead, you know. Concussion, I figure." She scanned her patient from head to toe. "And I don't like the look of that ankle."

All eyes followed her gaze to Cameron's right foot. No one had noticed it before, but the boot was twisted at an unnatural angle.

Cicero winced. "It's broken, all right. He's on his way home."

Somehow, that pronouncement percolated down to Cameron, who came awake with a howl. "No-o!"

"Just lie still," the doctor soothed. "I've got a splint in the ATV."

Cameron wept bitter tears of disappointment as the three guides immobilized his leg and placed him in the back of the vehicle.

"I blew it," he mourned. "Everest was so close I could see it in my sleep."

"It wasn't that close," Tilt told him mildly. "You were going in the next cut anyway."

"Hey, Crowley," Sneezy growled. "Ever consider a career in diplomacy?"

"I'm so stupid," moaned Cameron, covering his face with both hands.

"No!" Sammi exclaimed urgently. "Don't you get it? This is exactly how it's supposed to go! You went out in a blaze of glory, making a move nobody else saw! It's poetry!" She leaned over and kissed him on the forehead.

"It doesn't rhyme," was Tilt's comment.

Cicero regarded his nine remaining climbers. "Everybody's okay with this, right? Accidents happen."

Perry's mind screamed what his mouth didn't dare say: *Of course we're not okay with it! If this happens on Everest, it's going to mean a lot more than a broken ankle and a little concussion! It's going to be a four-thousand-foot drop down the Lhotse face!*

But aloud, he just murmured his assent along with the others.

Chris spoke up. "Cap, I know this is the wrong time to ask, but have you seen this?" He held out Todd's copy of the *National Daily*.

"I've read it," said Cicero, throwing a blanket

THE CONTEST

over Cameron. "I'm hoping it's just a one-time thing. But the fact is, we had a spy who might still be with us. So think twice before sharing your life story. Remember — Summit Athletic is sponsoring this expedition because it's good publicity. If they start getting more bad publicity than good, they could pull their funding and cancel the whole thing. Then nobody goes."

"And for God's sake tell them to stay off these boulders," added Dr. Oberman. "Especially this one!"

Cap started up the ATV, drowning out the doctor's suggestion.

Two words he would never say to a climber: *Stop climbing.*

## MEDICAL LOG — PSYCH PROFILES
### Interview with Samantha Moon

**Dr. Oberman:** *When you told Cameron his accident was like poetry, did you mean it?*
**Sammi:** *When you're a climber, that's what you are. To go down tackling a tough problem is as natural a thing as breathing. If you have to wash out, fine. But it shouldn't be because of a runny nose.*
**Dr. Oberman:** *If Cameron had fallen on his*

head, he could be dead right now. Would that be as natural as breathing?

**Sammi:** Why worry about something that didn't happen?

**Dr. Oberman:** People have died on Everest. 150 of them.

**Sammi:** That's what makes it extreme.

**Dr. Oberman:** You're not afraid of dying?

**Sammi:** I'm not going to die.

**Dr. Oberman:** How can you be so sure?

**Sammi:** Don't worry about me.

**Dr. Oberman:** If the possibility of dying is what makes it extreme, and you know for sure you're not going to die, then it's not really extreme, is it?

**Sammi:** Are we going to look at inkblots, or what?

THE CONTEST

# CHAPTER NINE

It happened just before midnight.

The quiet of the slumbering sports complex was shattered by a deafening clatter. It woke every sleeper.

Cap Cicero, still hopping into a pair of sweatpants, exploded into the hall with every ounce of the determination that had propelled him up the Matterhorn during the famous blizzard of 1998.

Perry appeared at the doorway of the room he shared with Tilt. "What was that?"

"Go back to bed!" roared Cicero, pounding down the hall. He wheeled around the corner, narrowly avoiding a collision with Sneezy.

"Calm down!" the cameraman/guide exclaimed. "Nobody's hurt."

Cicero looked past him to the utility closet. The door was open, and mops, brooms, and pails were scattered everywhere, along with bottles of detergent, floor wax, and bleach.

Cicero picked up a deck mop and stormed up and down the corridor, banging on doors.

"Maybe you're used to cushy guidance coun-

selors and child psychologists who think that bust-
ing up people's property is a cry for help. *I* work
in a place where there isn't any vandalism because every ounce of energy has to go to keeping yourself and your teammates alive! If Summit
came to me today and asked, 'Is your team ready
to go?' I'd have to say no. Because any idiot who
thinks it's fun to trash a broom closet has no place
on that mountain. And two weeks from now I'll
say the same thing and scrap this expedition.
Don't think I won't!"

He tossed the mop back into the closet and
stormed off.

"I'll wake up Maintenance," Sneezy called after him.

In the gloom of her dorm room, Sammi
Moon's face wore an oddly stricken expression. It
was not Cap's speech that had upset her; nor
was it even the grim prospect of having SummitQuest canceled.

She gazed across the sparsely furnished
space at Bryn's bed.

Her roommate was not there.

Dominic lay for a long time after the disturbance,
trying to empty his mind and will himself back to
sleep. This was weakness — on an expedition,

the ability to rest was as important as a good ice ax. Look at Chris. In the other bed, his brother was out like a light — and had been since thirty seconds after his head had hit the pillow.

The dim red glow of the digital clock on the nightstand read 2:11.

Resolutely, he got out of bed, pulled on jeans and a sweatshirt, and shrugged into a down ski jacket. Carrying his boots, he tiptoed out the door and down the hall to the darkened equipment room. He didn't risk a light — the locker room was directly across the courtyard from the security desk by reception. He felt around behind the door until his hand closed on a helmet lamp. He pulled it from its wall peg, then sat down on the floor, laced on his boots, and let himself out the side entrance into the frigid night.

Had Dominic turned on the light in the equipment room, he would have seen that there were Post-it notes — washout notes, they now called them — on four lockers. One of them was his.

He made his way over the rise and, when he was out of sight of the building, switched on the lamp. Light flooded the snowy terrain ahead of him. The trees cast unnaturally long shadows, like eerie pointers, showing the way down into the valley where the great mushroom stood. That had been his destination all along. When Dominic was restless, the answer was always the same: *Go climb something.*

All at once, he halted in his tracks and switched off the torch. Ahead of him, the mushroom was bathed in light. Someone was up there!

Staying in the cover of the trees, Dominic moved slowly forward.

The ATV was parked thirty feet away. On the back of it was a portable floodlight, its bright beam illuminating the "problem." Suspended there, dangling from the handhold on the underside of the crown, was Cap Cicero.

Dominic's first impulse was to turn on his heels and run for the complex. Instead, he stayed riveted to the spot. This was one of America's top alpinists, *climbing!*

He watched in awe as Cicero managed to gain a boot in the fissure. Then, hanging upside down, he literally created a hold out of thin air by wedging the side of his hand up against a quarter-inch ridge in the rock.

Dominic let out his breath and realized he'd been holding it. It was a brilliant move that required amazing wrist strength. Maybe one climber in a hundred could even have seen it was possible, let alone pulled it off. But, he noted, Cicero was still too far from the edge of the mush-

THE CONTEST

room to have a shot at the top. Spectacular as it was, this wasn't the move that would solve the problem.

Cicero retreated to the stem and began to climb down. Suddenly, he froze.

"Who's out there?"

Escape crossed Dominic's mind only briefly. Surely, he had no right to be here in the middle of the night. But somehow he had the feeling that a true climber would understand.

He stepped out into the light.

Cicero was surprised, and not pleasantly. "Alexis, are you crazy? It's two-thirty in the morning — " Then it occurred to him that there might be a confession coming. He descended the sloped pedestal and leaned against it to catch his breath. Dominic approached him, squinting against the powerful beam of the floodlight.

"So what's on your mind, kid?" Cicero prompted.

"I couldn't get back to sleep," Dominic admitted. "Sometimes my brain just goes wild, and I think about a million things one after the other. Tonight it kept coming back to this rock. So I thought I could — I don't know — study it or something."

Cicero flushed with anger. "Not on my watch! You're supposed to be in training, Mister, and — "

He stopped himself. Dominic *wasn't* in training anymore. Cicero himself had placed the Post-
it on the kid's locker. What was the point of
being mad at him? Even if it turned out that
Dominic was the SummitQuest vandal *and* responsible for leaking information to the *National
Daily*, he was leaving tomorrow. It didn't matter if
he was guilty of insomnia or a whole lot more; he
was *gone*.

Cicero inclined his head toward the boulder.
"It's a tough one," he agreed. "But to tackle it
solo, in the dark — "

In answer, Dominic clicked on his helmet
lamp. "And *you* came here alone," he pointed
out.

Cicero had to laugh. "What, you don't think
I've got the credentials?"

Dominic quoted from memory. "*Summer,
1998. Cap Cicero climbs every important peak
in the Alps in six weeks.*"

"I had good weather," the team leader said,
embarrassed.

Dominic clambered up the pedestal and
worked his way over to the stem of the mushroom.

Cicero looked at the sky in exasperation. "I
thought I was speaking English. It must have been
Cantonese." Yet he couldn't help but watch as the

young climber moved efficiently up the problem. "You won't make that handhold," he predicted. "You haven't got the wingspan. Here — " He shinnied up the stem to Dominic and positioned himself to provide a platform to get the boy within reach of the fissure.

With a grunt of thanks, Dominic was able to make it to the cleft in the rock, using Cicero's knees as a stepping-off point. Then, carefully but with confidence, he duplicated the team leader's move. As he hung there, upside down, the helmet lamp fell off his head and shattered on the pedestal below.

"See?" said Cicero. "If it wasn't for my light, you'd be in the dark right now. Alone. Wait a second, and I'll give you a hand getting down."

"I can do it." The voice was not even strained. Slowly, exhibiting remarkable muscle control, Dominic reversed the move. But instead of swinging back down to the artificial ledge provided by Cicero's knees, he launched himself directly at the stem, catching on and sticking, Spiderman-style.

Cicero replayed the reverse move and dismount with wide eyes. Of course it wasn't impossible; he had just witnessed it. But someone of Dominic's size should not have that kind of strength, not to mention the guts to try something like that.

"Get in the car!" he said gruffly.

As they drove off in the ATV, Cicero noticed that Dominic didn't face front until the boulder was out of sight.

Cicero fretted over the steering wheel. Dominic was cut, finished, gone. And yet the team leader couldn't get the kid out of his head.

He thought, *Is it wrong to let this boy stay in boot camp when he has absolutely no chance of making the team? Is it fair to keep him around just because I like him and I want to see what he'll do next?*

The next morning, the nine candidates awoke to find only three Post-it notes in the equipment room. Three more Everest hopefuls were going home.

Dominic Alexis was not one of them.

THE CONTEST

# CHAPTER TEN

Chris, Bryn, Tilt, Sammi, Perry, and Dominic were still standing. Somewhere, Ethan Zaph made seven. By the end of the month, three of them would be gone.

The Summit complex, scene of budding friendships, excited chatter, and screaming arguments, became as silent as a tomb. As Everest moved within reach, the candidates retreated inside themselves and focused on their training with the concentration and tunnel vision only athletes understand.

Sammi explained it in an interview for the Web site. "Last week, we were supporting one another to get this far. Now, all of a sudden, it's me me me."

"There's too much at stake to be nice to people," Tilt agreed.

"Like he'd know anything about being nice to people," Chris muttered under his breath.

But as the front-runner, confident, affable Chris was feeling the pressure more than anyone. He had watched Ethan Zaph become a star by summiting Everest. Now it was finally his turn. His

Dead Sea sand could be headed for the top of the world. A SummitQuest spot was his for the taking — but also his for the losing if he slacked off.

"My brother hasn't talked to me in three days," Dominic said on camera. "But that's okay. He hasn't talked to anybody else, either."

Even the normally boisterous Tilt seemed subdued. In part, it was an effort to avoid angering Cap this close to the moment of decision. But it was also from just plain nervousness. To him, this was more than an expedition; it was his future. Mess up, and it was back home, back to the paper routes, back to his life as a nobody. Who knew when he'd get another chance like this? Maybe never.

So he kept his mouth shut while Cicero ran everybody ragged. A speed climb? Great idea, Cap. Of course the slave driver didn't mention that they'd be doing it on Amethyst Peak, a full sprint up a thirteen-thousand-foot mountain. Eight grueling hours on the ascent, plus three more going down — get this — in the *dark*. No helmet lamps. No ropes. Nothing. A guy could break a leg and cost himself a chance at the summit that *really* counted.

"Congratulations," Cicero told them as they lay gasping at the end. "You've just put in a typical day's work in the Himalayas." Never mind that the whole Everest route was fixed with ropes, and the closest thing to free climbing they'd be doing was the walk along the yak trail into base camp. Biggest challenge — not stepping in the yak doo. Sure, Cap. Anything you say.

And when they had to wait an hour for Perry to catch up, Tilt didn't say a word about that, either. Only Cicero knew why Perry was still alive in this thing when he wasn't fit to carry Tilt's crampons.

Mealtimes were the worst. With none of the candidates saying much, there were plenty of empty spaces for Cicero to fill with boring memories of his alpine career: "Did I ever tell you about the time on Gasherbrum . . . ?" "Once, I was climbing in the Andes and there was this avalanche. . . ." "I'll never forget the night I was trapped in a crevasse on the Vinson Massif in Antarctica. . . ."

The others actually seemed to like those stupid climbing stories, Dominic especially. The runt's eyes lit up every time Cicero opened his mouth. And even Tilt had to admit that Cicero's Greatest Hits was still better than having to listen to Sneezy's dumb jokes or Dr. Oberman's probing questions: "And how does that make you feel?"

*It makes me feel like I want you to shut up.*

To minimize his chances of combusting in front of Cicero or his guides, Tilt had thrown himself into his schoolwork. The complex had a computer lab where the Everest hopefuls could keep up with their classes via the Internet. These days, all of them were clocking major time there. It was a way to avoid conversation. Even Chris, the flunk-out champion of the group, was a student all of a sudden. Not that Chris was going to have any trouble getting a full ride to any college in the country. Cicero loved him. He was going up Everest no matter what. But he wouldn't be the youngest. Not if Tilt Crowley had anything to say about it!

Tilt slipped up only once in front of Cicero. It happened on yesterday's ascent. Low on the mountain, there was a steep rock scramble that led through a narrow limestone crevice — almost like a vertical tunnel in the route. It was simple enough for a real alpinist, but Perry was obsessed with his lines and bolts and pitons. The guy would top rope a flight of stairs. Free climbing spooked him.

He made it up the tunnel part okay, but at the opening he just froze. Either he couldn't find the foothold, or he just couldn't compel his body to heave itself out into the open.

THE CONTEST

Cicero was about twenty feet away, talking to Sneezy, who was shooting for the Web site. Tilt could have reached out and hauled Perry up by the collar, but didn't it make sense to show Cicero that he had a climber who was either too uncoordinated or too chicken to execute a maneuver straight out of Mountaineering 101?

Cicero quickly took in the situation. "Give him a hand, Crowley."

Tilt could have done it, *should* have done it, and the incident would have passed unnoticed. But then came the frustration, the anger that some person, some *force* was protecting this mediocre climber from the washout that should have happened weeks ago. And Tilt couldn't hold back: "Maybe you should ask his *guardian angel* to come save him!"

The expedition leader glared at him. "I told you to help him out!"

Tilt yanked Perry up beside him. The red-haired boy brushed himself off. "Thanks."

Tilt didn't answer. He was in equal measure enraged and terrified by the expression on Cicero's face — the I'm-writing-it-all-down-and-this-is-going-to-cost-you look he had seen so many times before.

That night, to stay out of Cicero's face, he studied so hard for a science test that he scored

100 percent. If he didn't get to go to Everest, he reflected, at least he was turning himself into a genius in the process. And a hermit.

That was the plan. Keep quiet. Speak only when spoken to.

And pray.

### MEDICAL LOG — PSYCH PROFILES
#### Interview with Norman Crowley

**Dr. Oberman:** *Tilt — is that a climbing nickname?*

**Tilt:** *No, ma'am. It's a name I got because I used to love playing old-fashioned pinball machines.*

**Dr. Oberman:** *Is mountaineering a Crowley family sport?*

**Tilt:** *My parents aren't into sports.*

**Dr. Oberman:** *But you are?*

**Tilt:** *Just climbing. It's everything to me. I'm nothing without it.*

**Dr. Oberman:** *What about Everest? Think you'll make the team?*

**Tilt:** *Hope so. I'm really counting on it.*

**Dr. Oberman:** *What's your attitude toward your fellow climbers here at boot camp?*

**Tilt:** *Everybody's great. I want to make it, but I wish them all luck.*

THE CONTEST

**Dr. Oberman:** And I'm talking to the real Tilt Crowley?

**Tilt:** What do you mean?

**Dr. Oberman:** The word around here is that you're abusive, unfriendly, uncooperative —

**Tilt:** I understand. Really, I do. Climbing is very intense, and to be up against a competitive group like this — who wouldn't be scared of guys like Chris Alexis and Ethan Zaph? I guess I come on a little strong. . . . Do you think I should apologize to the others?

# CHAPTER ELEVEN

*Crash!*

Bryn came awake in the usual way, the way she had come to dread. First, a murky semiconsciousness, and then dawning horror. Horror that it had happened again.

There she stood, pajama-clad and barefoot in the TV lounge, surrounded by shattered glass. The trophy case — destroyed. The soapstone Eskimo sculpture — broken in half where it had been thrown through the doors. Where *she* had thrown it —

"What's going on out there?"

Cicero's voice galvanized her into action. She ran out of the lounge, avoiding the shards of glass with high-stepping feet.

A commotion in the dormitory hall. Doors opening. Voices. She began to panic. She would never get back to her room without being seen.

*Don't let me get caught now! Not when I'm so close!*

The laundry room! She ducked through the door.

*That was stupid. They might look in here.*

THE CONTEST

Feeling like she was losing control of an already absurd situation, she climbed into an industrial-sized dryer and pulled the door almost closed.

The sounds that followed had become familiar: footsteps and groggy voices; Cicero's tirade. She couldn't make out all his words, but the message was obvious: If he ever found out who was behind this vandalism . . .

*But it isn't vandalism!*

The timing was everything. She had to hit the gap — the lull after the SummitQuest people had gone back to bed but before Maintenance arrived to clean up the mess. What a skill to become expert at!

*Just be grateful nobody decided to throw in a midnight load of laundry.*

She crept down the hall, her feet barely touching the floor. Her eyes were focused like laser beams on the door to the room she shared with Sammi. Climber's habit. You never take your eyes off the destination — the next pitch, the next ledge, the next camp.

She let herself in and paused, calming her racing heart as she waited for her eyes to get used to the dark. She had made it. She had pulled it off. Again.

The light clicked on, and there was Sammi, watching her intently. "We need to talk."

"Somebody threw the black igloo into the trophy case," Bryn explained, struggling to keep the panic out of her voice. "It's smashed."

"I know," said Sammi. "You'd better get your brush. There's still some glass in your hair."

As soon as she heard the words, Bryn knew it was over. That sculpture had shattered her Everest dream as surely as it had the glass of the trophy case. She was going home. But what was home, anyway? A place to watch Mom and Dad snipe at each other through their lawyers instead of directly? To witness them dividing up the assets, the last of which would be *her*? The irony was that her parents, who had fought so hard over SummitQuest, weren't going to live happily ever after just because she was the next washout.

Sammi picked up the phone on the nightstand. "This is Sammi Moon. Could you ask Cap to come to room fourteen? Thanks." She faced Bryn. "Before he gets here, answer this one question: What's your payoff? What are you getting out of this? I mean, I'm good, but you're better. That spot was all sewn up for you. Why would you throw it away just to smash a little glass?"

Bryn was so downcast that she couldn't even look at her roommate. Her entire reply was addressed to the weave of the carpet.

"I was five years old when I started sleepwalking. I don't even remember it. Just the stuff that happened because of it — the window I broke, the stairs I fell down, the special doctor I had to see. I'm not even sure when it stopped, just that it did. It was ancient history — until I came here. Honest, I'm in bed, and then suddenly I'm in the middle of a demolition derby — busted dishes, the ruins of a lamp, a tangle of mops and pails. And I can't remember how I got there."

Sammi was wide-eyed. "You have to tell Cap! A sleepwalking climber! Here it's a broken trophy case; on E it's a ten-thousand-foot drop!"

Bryn tried to explain. "You don't understand! This isn't a part of my life. It's just boot camp. It's like living in a pressure cooker. I know once I get away from here the sleepwalking will stop!"

"But what if it doesn't?"

"It will! There's something freaky about this place — the stress, the competition, the feeling that your every move is being watched. You make friends and then you have to stomp all over them before they stomp all over you."

"I love climbing," Sammi agreed, "but this is no way to live. By the time it's over, we're all going to be like Tilt."

"But once the team is set, everything will be back to normal," Bryn persisted. "And I *know* I won't be sleepwalking anymore!"

Sammi was silent for a long time. "I want to win that spot," she said finally. "But not like this."

"We can both make it," Bryn enthused. "It's a long shot, but it's *possible*. Or maybe you'll get picked over me. Cap's unpredictable. Who knows what's in his mind? Perry and Dominic are still here. Who would have believed that?"

There was a sharp rap at the door. "What's going on in there?" came Cicero's gruff voice. "Are you guys okay?"

Sammi and Bryn locked eyes. The decision was made in that instant.

"Is everything all right, Cap?" Sammi called.

"You couldn't ask me that over the phone?" was the roared reply.

"Sorry," Sammi apologized. "Did you find out who broke the case?"

"And stop the fun so soon?" snarled the team leader. "No, I want to give the person a chance to spray-paint graffiti on the Khumbu Icefall! Go back to sleep!"

They listened to him stomp away.

Bryn's eyes filled with tears. "I can't believe you did that for me."

"I can hardly believe it myself," said Sammi Moon.

# CHAPTER TWELVE

### MEDICAL LOG — PSYCH PROFILES
#### Interview with Cap Cicero

**Cicero:** Come on, Andrea, is this really necessary? I'm not one of the kids.

**Dr. Oberman:** I heard you on that three-hour conference call. They could hear you in Denver.

**Cicero:** Sometimes I say things with emphasis.

**Dr. Oberman:** The final cut is Friday. I'm guessing you were making a last-ditch effort to unload a certain climber.

**Cicero:** You'll never know how hard I tried. I don't want him. Even the kid doesn't want to go. I was as good as told that the whole expedition depends on it.

**Dr. Oberman:** So that's it, then. You did all you could.

**Cicero:** I always said I'd never put an unqualified climber on that mountain. I'd scrap the whole thing first. Do you think it's easy to admit to yourself that you're not as honorable as you thought you were?

**Dr. Oberman:** What do you mean?

EVEREST

**Cicero:** A fifteen-year-old boy might die half a world away from his family and everything he knows. I could prevent that. But apparently, all I care about is having another crack at Everest.

**Dr. Oberman:** Aren't you forgetting something? That fifteen-year-old is going to have a guide who's the best in the business. If anyone can get Perry to the top, it's you.

**Cicero:** A guide can't stop altitude sickness or a falling chunk of ice.

**Dr. Oberman:** Those things are acts of God. They'd have the same effect on the most skilled climber in the world. Summit picked you because you're number one, because they know that their kids will be as safe as it's possible to be on a Himalayan peak.

**Cicero:** Okay, but just don't ask how it makes me feel.

**Dr. Oberman:** If anything, this does your job for you. That's one less spot you have to pick. Will you be ready to announce the team on Friday?

**Cicero:** I'm ready now.

The final team was unveiled late Wednesday afternoon, two days early. Ethan Zaph, Christian Alexis, Bryn Fiedler, and Perry Noonan would be

THE CONTEST

traveling to Nepal as Cap Cicero's SummitQuest expedition. Sammi Moon, Tilt Crowley, and Dominic Alexis were going home.

It was never easy to tell a climber, young or old, that he or she didn't measure up. But Cicero was actually looking forward to his meeting with Tilt. He had even prepared a speech: *You're a great climber but a lousy person. I wouldn't put you on my team if you were the last kid on Earth.*

And when the moment came, the Tilt Crowley who sat across the desk from him wasn't the brash, selfish bully Cicero had come to know and dislike. He was just a heartbroken fourteen-year-old who was having his life's dream snatched away.

"Crowley, you've got some growing up to do," was all Cicero could manage. "Sorry it didn't work out."

Tilt stumbled out of the office, stunned and devastated, and managed to fumble his way into his room to pack.

It was too late to make it to Denver to catch flights home, so Sammi, Tilt, and Dominic were not scheduled to leave until morning. The last night at the Summit complex was not going to be a pleasant one for them.

Tilt didn't show up at dinner. Sammi and Dominic were there, but without much appetite. Nei-

ther had expected to make it, but the disappointment was still keenly felt.

"I'm sleeping in the TV lounge tonight," Perry
said feelingly. "Tilt's going to strangle me in my
bed."

In truth, if there was anyone more shaken than
Tilt, it was Perry. The news that he had made the
Everest team had shocked him to the core. Oh,
sure, it had been obvious, as he survived cut after
cut, that there was something more than talent
keeping him in the running. But never had he expected it to go this far. Like the moment in a bad
dream where you're conscious enough to know
you're going to wake up before the really
hideous part, he had always relied on Cicero to
put an end to this. And now he was on his way to
climb a killer mountain.

That night, he sat in the lounge, surfing old re-
runs on TV until around midnight, when Dr. Oberman caught him there.

"You're in training, Perry. You know you
should be in bed."

"Right," said Perry. "I was just on my way."

She regarded him intently. "And congratulations."

For a moment, he looked at her as if she
were speaking Greek. Then, "Thanks, Andrea.
Thanks."

THE CONTEST

She paused. "You know, no one can make you do something you don't want to do."

Perry nodded slowly. "Good night." She had obviously never met Uncle Joe.

If Perry had expected rage, bullying, and abuse, it was not to be. In fact, Tilt was already in bed and did not address a single word to him.

All night, Perry could hear muffled sobs coming from the other side of the room. And if Tilt had not been so wrapped up in his own misery, he would have been able to detect similar sounds coming from Perry.

It was a curious paradox that one roommate should be crying because he wasn't going, and the other because he was.

Dominic zipped up his duffel bag and swung it over his shoulder. "I'll see you in a few days," he said to his brother.

Tomorrow, the team would be flying up to the Alaskan panhandle for a practice ascent. After that, they would return home for three weeks of rest and preparation for the trip to Kathmandu and the ultimate adventure.

Chris put an arm around his younger brother's slender shoulders. "You know, Dom, I thought it was crazy, you saving all those wrappers and caps. But I'm really glad you were here with me.

Is there anything you want me to take to the summit?"

Dominic grinned ruefully. "Yeah — me."

"You'll get your shot," Chris promised. "You're a great climber. There's nothing wrong with you that time won't take care of. Try not to hold it against Cap."

Dominic looked surprised. "It's been the greatest thing in my life, training with Cap Cicero. I'll never forget this month." He opened the door. "I've got a plane to catch."

Outside, Bryn was helping Sammi load her luggage into the Summit van.

"It's called cliff jumping," Sammi was explaining brightly. "Caleb did it last year in the Canadian Rockies. You're on skis, but it's not a real run, so you have to jump from snow patch to snow patch. If you hit rock, the wipeouts can be nasty. It's pretty extreme."

Bryn was all choked up. "I'll never forget what you did for me."

Sammi shrugged. "You climbers are too obsessed with mountains, mountains, mountains. There's plenty of adventure out there. I'll find something cool to do." She embraced her roommate. "Sleep tight," she said meaningfully.

"I will," Bryn promised.

Tilt was already in the van, eyes staring

THE CONTEST

straight forward, his face a thundercloud. He said good-bye to no one, and no one said good-bye to him.

Sneezy's video camera rolled on as Sammi and Dominic pulled the door shut. The footage was shaky and of low quality. The cameraman was having his usual hard time watching candidates on their way home. To make matters worse, Lenny Tkakzuk would be driving the van into Denver. So he would be seeing the three disappointed climbers all the way to their airplanes. It was extra agony for a tenderhearted guide.

The drive was shattering — two hours of nothing but mountains, the last thing a failed climber wanted to think about. Dominic tried to envision the scenery of Kansas or maybe Nebraska. But the winding Colorado highway offered up snowcapped peak after snowcapped peak, stinging reminders of what had been so close, but had slipped away from them.

He listened to the never-ending scores and analysis from the all-sports station that the radio was tuned to, mingled with the tinny whine escaping from Sammi's headphones. The only other sound in the van was Tilt's breathing, steady, but too heavy, like a bull about to charge.

Tilt's temper snapped about an hour into the drive. In a single motion, he had the tape out of the player and out the window before Sammi could exclaim, "Hey! That was Garbage!"

"Now it's roadkill," muttered Tilt.

Dominic slipped out of his belt and positioned himself between the two of them on the bench seat.

"You're going to pay for that!" Sammi raged.

"Who's going to make me?" sneered Tilt. "The shrimp?"

"Come on, guys," pleaded Sneezy, trying to watch the road and keep an eye on his charges at the same time. "I know this isn't an easy trip —"

Sammi fixed her furious gaze on Tilt. "You think because I'm a girl, I'm not going to put you through that back window?"

Tilt seemed to relish the chance to blow off steam. "You think because you're a girl, I'm not going to hope you try?"

"Leave her alone," ordered Dominic.

"Shut up!" chorused the combatants.

Sneezy pulled the van over to the shoulder, stopping in a spray of gravel. He turned in his seat. "Cut it out!!"

They were momentarily shocked into silence. No one had ever heard the affable Sneezy raise his voice in anger. It was in that lull that the announcement came over the Sports Report:

"It was learned today that Ethan Zaph, the

teen who conquered Everest last year, has pulled out of Summit Athletic's SummitQuest expedition. In a case of 'Been there, done that,' Zaph has signed on with This Way Up, a team that's planning a double ascent of Everest and nearby Lhotse. Zaph, the youngest ever to bag the world's tallest peak, promises this year's climb will be made without the help of supplemental oxygen."

Everybody froze. The news was so stunning that it brought on a disorientation. The four occupants of the van couldn't even remember what they had been fighting about scant seconds before. The whole world had shifted. The final team was no longer locked in.

Sneezy's cell phone rang, but he made no move for it. It rang again.

"Answer it," breathed Tilt.

The conversation was brief. "Got it, Cap." Sneezy threw the van into a U-turn, squealing across four lanes of highway. They were already doing seventy when the left front tire flattened and pulverized Sammi's Garbage tape.

# CHAPTER THIRTEEN

Cap Cicero was screaming now. "You want me to do *what?*"

Tony Devlin tried to be calm. "When Ethan Zaph quit the expedition, we lost our star, the guy who was going to draw attention to our team. The only way to regain that spotlight is to break his record — to summit a kid even younger. Or the youngest girl. Or both."

"All right," said Cicero. "If anybody has a chance, Bryn does. She's Himalayan quality."

"We need a sure thing," Devlin insisted. "Or as close to it as we can get. We have to pack that team with home runs."

"I'll take Sammi Moon in Zaph's spot," agreed Cicero. "I didn't really want to cut her anyway."

"What about Tilt Crowley?" asked Devlin. "He's like a guaranteed record."

"He's like a guaranteed head case," Cicero shot back. "We live in close quarters up there. A disruption can be death — and I'm not speaking figuratively."

THE CONTEST

"The board of directors thinks you should give him another look."

"All right, I'll take him," Cicero said defiantly. "In Perry Noonan's spot."

Devlin didn't blink. "Perry goes, no matter what."

"Well, I'm not taking Crowley over Moon."

"You don't have to," said Devlin. "You're going to take him over Chris Alexis."

Cicero stood up so violently that his chair went flying. "Chris Alexis is the best climber I've got! I *need* him. He'll be like an extra guide on Everest."

Devlin was firm. "He's too old to break the record. We can't put our resources behind a kid who isn't going to get us the attention we need. As Ethan Zaph's teammate, he was fine. But now the rules have changed. He's no use to us."

Cicero took a deep breath as Devlin's words sank in. Part of him wanted to lash out for the expedition's sake and poor Chris's, too. But Cicero had been climbing far too long not to understand the way things worked. It took a lot of money to put an alpinist atop Everest. A sponsor didn't ante up that kind of cash for the love of mountaineering. They did it for the glory, the prestige, and mostly for the advertising. If Summit wanted a record, Cicero had to try to deliver, even if he thought the whole business stank.

"I'm surprised you're not asking me to take Dominic," he muttered resentfully. "The kid's barely out of diapers."

"We considered it," said Devlin in all seriousness. "To put a thirteen-year-old on the summit would be an unbelievable coup. But we decided he's just too small. He wouldn't have a real chance to get to the top. Not like Tilt."

But even then Cicero couldn't commit. Devlin was still protesting as the team leader showed him out of the office.

"Don't worry," Cicero assured him. "We'll be ready for Alaska tomorrow."

"Taking which kids?" probed Devlin.

"You'll know that as soon as I do."

Cicero went through the day as if in a daze. He had led dozens of expeditions before, full of rich and powerful clients who had paid tens of thousands of dollars to have a crack at Everest or one of the other eight-thousand-meter peaks. The infighting! The egos! The one-upmanship! But none of those trips had created the kind of headaches he was having over this one.

It came down to this: All his instincts told him to avoid Perry Noonan and Tilt Crowley. He was

THE CONTEST

already stuck with Perry. And now it looked as if he would have to take Tilt, too. He thought back to the kids who had disappeared in the prior rounds of cuts. Surely there was someone in there who was young enough and able enough to take instead of Crowley!

After twenty-seven days of nonstop training, the Summit complex suddenly saw leisure time, and lots of it. The van with the former washouts returned to find no climbing exercises, no hikes, no drills — just confusion. The final team was set — or was it? What was going on?

The returnees filled them in — the famous Ethan Zaph was a scratch.

The six waited for news at first, but Cicero's office door remained shut. Eventually, Sneezy and Dr. Oberman shooed them away. But no one chose to visit the gym or the indoor climbing wall. No one could concentrate on anything but the suspense of the moment. They wandered the building like tourists, rubbernecking as though they were seeing the complex for the first time.

Except Dominic.

Cicero was still in his office when he spied the boy trudging through the snow down into the valley. He could have been going anywhere, but Cicero knew his destination instantly. It was where he would have been going in Dominic's place, where any bred-in-the-bone climber would go — the mushroom boulder, the unsolved problem.

With a sense of urgency, Cicero raced up to the observation lounge on the top floor of the building. The plush suite, used for receptions and high-level corporate meetings, had telescopes mounted all around the panoramic windows. The westernmost had a clear view of that valley.

He peered into the eyepiece and fiddled with the knob until the Mushroom came into focus. Then he zoomed in. Sure enough, there was Dominic, right on schedule.

The boy didn't climb right away, but sat there, leaning against the lopsided pedestal at the base, three times his height. He was looking up, studying the problem. At last, he rose, rubbing his hands together — a rock climber's gesture. He ascended the pedestal and then the stem, searching for handholds on the underside of the massive top slab.

Once again, the team leader found himself completely absorbed. "Come down, kid," he murmured aloud. "It's just not there."

And Dominic did come down. But only as far as the pedestal. He paused for a second, took three running steps, and launched himself off the highest point of the base, up and out — a dyno,

THE CONTEST

the ultimate rock climber's move. For a split second, his slim body hung in midair, twenty-five feet off the ground. Then, his hands came out of nowhere and clamped onto a small knob on the side of the mushroom cap. An instant later, he was on the top.

Cicero very nearly cheered. The move was as daring as it was brilliant. If Dominic hadn't stuck that hold, he'd be on the way to the hospital right now! The kid had solved the unsolvable. And he did it just because he refused to let it beat him.

Too young. Too small. These things would disqualify other climbers. But not Dominic, because Dominic always found a way. And if the boy didn't deserve Everest yet, maybe Everest deserved him.

The team came together in his mind: Bryn Fiedler, Sammi Moon, Perry Noonan, and Dominic Alexis.

No Ethan Zaph, no Chris Alexis, two girls, a guy who didn't even want to go, and a middle-school kid.

The gods must be crazy!

The farewell scene was replicated in the Alexis brothers' room, but this time it was Chris who was packing to leave.

Dominic was distraught. "I can't believe Cap

did this to you, Chris. I should tell him to stuff it!"

"Are you crazy?" Chris exclaimed. "You don't owe me that much loyalty! When he cut you, I never said boo."

"I deserved to get cut!" Dominic insisted. "Not you. You're the best of all of us!"

"But I'm over the hill," Chris said bitterly. "I'll be sixteen soon."

"Cap's a jerk!" Dominic raged. "I'll never respect him again. Tilt wasn't right about much, but he was right about Cap."

His brother almost managed a smile. "If there's one consolation in all this, it's seeing Tilt Crowley get cut for the second time in two days."

"You watch out for him," Dominic warned. "When he gets mad, he's nastier than usual."

Chris undid the leather strap from around his neck and pressed the small vial of Dead Sea sand into his brother's hand. "It's all up to you now, Dom. I want this left on the summit. From the bottom of the world to the top. That hasn't changed."

"It's changed because you're not going to be there." Dominic was close to tears.

"You make sure you get there," Chris said bravely. "And back down again. Remember — summiting is optional, but coming home is mandatory."

THE CONTEST

# CHAPTER FOURTEEN

For the past month, the Summit complex had been their universe. Now, suddenly, jarringly, the SummitQuest team was on the move.

Harried preparation. Pack your personal gear. Hurry up. No, you don't need sunblock; you're going to Alaska in February. Ice ax — check. Crampons — check. Helmet lamp — check. Inner gloves, outer mitts. Everybody into the van. We're late! Drive to Denver. Fly to Juneau. Load all the gear into the helicopter. And off into the air again.

Through the window of the chopper, Dominic watched the Juneau airport fall away. Even at one o'clock in the afternoon, it was dusk this far north. Not that you could see the sky. A heavy overcast was dropping a fine, hazy mist. A few miles inland and that turned to snow — not heavy, but steady. After the spectacular blue cloudlessness of the Colorado mountains, this place seemed as alien as outer space.

"When's the weather going to clear?" Perry asked nervously.

Cicero laughed. "People have gotten old waiting for the weather to clear up here."

Sneezy had his face pressed against the glass. "Look! There it is — Lucifer's Claw!"

"All I see is snow," commented Bryn.

Then, like a 3-D Pixelgram, it appeared out of the squall — a tall, misshapen, ice-covered spike, stark and massive.

"Extreme," breathed Sammi. It was the highest compliment she could pay.

The helicopter began to descend.

At 9,500 feet, Lucifer's Claw was less than a third the height of Everest. It wasn't even as tall as some of the peaks they had tackled in the Colorado training ground. But with a base just short of four thousand feet above sea level, it represented more than a vertical mile of ascent. Most important of all, they would encounter many of the same obstacles that the expedition would face in the Himalayas — glaciers, crevasses, ice walls, cornices, and all the bad weather a mountaineer could hope to use as preparation for the top of the world.

It was three degrees below zero when the pilot unloaded the team and their gear onto the Atkinson Glacier at the base of Lucifer's Claw.

"I guess you bring a lot of climbers out here," Perry commented.

THE CONTEST

The pilot shrugged. "There were these three Germans back in the early 1990s. Never did find out what happened to them." And he clambered back into the chopper and disappeared into the murky sky.

Dr. Oberman put a hand on Perry's shoulder. "Don't look so terrified. He was kidding."

But away from the comforts and conveniences of the Summit complex, there was no time to be scared. First priority was shelter; then food.

All at once, Dominic was grateful for their forced camp-out during the snowstorm at boot camp. The tents went up efficiently, the propane stoves were assembled and burning. It was now pitch-black outside. Dominic's watch read two-thirty.

They ate by the light of a small campfire — a luxury. At the high camp the next night, there would be nothing to burn. Cicero went over the plan.

"If you climb your whole life, you're never going to have a tougher day than the one we've got tomorrow. We're going to get up that wall, and it's all or nothing, because there's nowhere to stop until we hit the south shoulder at eight thousand feet. We'll sleep there, summit the next morning, and shoot straight down to meet the helicopter to take us out of here. We'll be in the dark a lot of the time, so guard your helmet lamp with your life."

As Dominic concentrated on the team leader's words, he became aware of a wetness on his cheeks. He sat there, expressionless, the tears pouring from his eyes. He'd been on the move for over ten hours, yet it was only now starting to sink in that he'd made it. His disbelief and his sympathy for Chris's pain had left no room for him to feel joy. Here, in the dark and blowing snow of a remote Alaskan glacier, he finally had the chance to celebrate himself. The journey that had begun with him chasing his brother's vial of Dead Sea sand down the parking ramp at the 7-Eleven had brought him here.

And the next stop was Everest.

Perry Noonan's climber's Rolex, another gift from Uncle Joe, read 2:15 A.M. when he raced out of the tent he shared with Dominic to answer nature's call. Of all the things he hated about climbing — and there were many — the bathroom situation was the worst.

With the fire out, it was dark. No, that wasn't strong enough. It was inky, suffocating black. There might have been moonlight somewhere, but behind fourteen layers of overcast it wasn't doing him much good.

He took a careful step, then a few more. In this visibility, to stray too far from camp was suicide. Another step — and suddenly he was down and sliding.

It was like no terror he had ever experienced to be falling, out of control, when he was completely blind. Then it was over. With a whump at the base of his spine, he came up against hard rock or ice.

A quick inventory. No broken bones, everything still attached. He got on all fours and began to crawl. He was out of the hole in a few seconds — at least he was enough of a climber to accomplish that. He was lucky. As near as he could tell, he had fallen into the gap between two chunks of glacial ice, each about the size of a refrigerator. If that had been a crevasse on Everest, he'd be dead already. Or worse — trapped alive and waiting for death. It had happened many times before, to amateurs and top climbers alike. It would no doubt happen many times again.

It took him twenty-five minutes to locate the tent in the dark. He had been a grand total of twelve feet away. Shaking with relief, he crawled into his sleeping bag and huddled there, trying not to wake Dominic with his ragged breathing.

It was then that he realized there was something he had forgotten to do. But another bathroom trek was out of the question.

# CHAPTER FIFTEEN

Five A.M., when Cap Cicero woke the team, was no different from the dead of night — pitch-black, ice-cold, and snowing.

By a meager fire, the climbers melted snow for a breakfast of hot chocolate and instant oatmeal. No one had much of an appetite. After four weeks of preparation, there was climbing to be done, and this was not a drill.

They struck down the camp. All gear — tents, stoves, sleeping bags — was to be carried on their backs to be reused at their next stop, nearly a vertical mile above them. It was time to don wind suits and Gore-Tex face masks and mitts, and to strap on crampons — boot attachments featuring twelve sharp prongs. The metal spikes bit into blue glacial ice as they shouldered their packs.

The mission could not have been simpler. First, a half-mile hike to the base of Lucifer's Claw, skirting dangerous crevasses. It made the hair stand up on the back of Perry's neck. If last night's tumble had been into any of these, there would be no Perry Noonan today.

THE CONTEST

Once they reached the mountain, they were vertical almost immediately, ascending the steep wall.

The front points of their crampons jabbed into the frozen shell covering the rock. Then a swing each from ice axes in both hands. Pull yourself up and start over again. *Kick. Kick. Thunk. Thunk.* To Dominic, the rhythm became almost as familiar as his own heartbeat.

They climbed, roped together in pairs: Dominic and Bryn, Sammi and Dr. Oberman, Cicero and Perry. The expedition leader figured it would take all his talent as a guide to keep Perry from falling behind. The red-haired boy was nervously securing himself with ice screws every few feet.

"For God's sake, Noonan," Cicero called impatiently, "if you put one more piece of hardware in that ice, you're going to magnetize the whole mountain!"

Sneezy was the odd man out. He climbed solo, taking miles of video of the ghosts cast by helmet lamps on the icy south wall of Lucifer's Claw.

The sun rose at around ten o'clock, or at least, as Bryn put it, "It's bright enough to watch the snow blow in our faces."

They celebrated with water and Summit bars.

The ice was thick and strong, and between the bite of ice screws and the front points of their crampons, the climbers were able to pause for a break while hanging off the wall. It felt something like comfort. Cicero and Sneezy changed positions. Now the expedition leader was solo.

By that time, Dominic had lost track of how many pitches they'd climbed. It had to be at least a dozen. But they were not yet even halfway up.

Within a few hours, it was dark again.

The month of training held fatigue at bay for a long time. But when it finally came, it was crushing. All at once, the effort of swinging an ax seemed to call for superhuman strength. Kicking crampon points into the ice felt like blasting through armor plating. Their feet weighed sixty tons. Even Perry's boundless energy to stud the mountain with screws disappeared. Sneezy had to remind him to place a belay station every thirty feet.

Conversation dwindled down to the bare essentials — "almost there," "hold this," "tired." Then even the essentials were no longer essential. After that, the only sounds were wind, grunts of effort, and the crunch of ice axes and crampons.

When their helmet lamps illuminated the rounding of the wall that marked the start of the

THE CONTEST

shoulder, Dominic and Bryn sped up, a new vitality coursing through them at the sight of their goal.

"We're there?" puffed Sammi off to their left. "We're close?"

"Slow down," ordered Dr. Oberman. "The angle of the shoulder has a foreshortening effect. It looks closer than it really is."

Sure enough, an hour of backbreaking work later, the shoulder appeared no nearer.

They slogged on until Cicero front-pointed past them in a show of speed and stamina that was breathtaking. Above them, he disappeared over the rounding of the icy rock face. Once on level ground, he slung a top rope around a boulder and dropped it down the wall. Sidestepping with their crampons, the climbers converged on it. One by one, they ascended the line and joined the expedition leader on the shoulder.

Bryn, Sammi, Perry, and Dominic collapsed in an untidy heap. But the guides soon had them up again.

"Now's the time you *don't* rest," barked Cicero. "Not until the tents are up and dinner's on."

Their bodies had been pushed to the limit for eleven and a half hours. The altitude gauge on Perry's watch read 8,063 feet. The air temperature was thirty-seven degrees below zero.

Their destination was an unnatural-looking place, even in the forbidding environs of Lucifer's Claw. The mountain's towering walls were gray-white with frost and snow. But the shoulder was naked black rock, swept clean by a relentless wind.

From the center of this obsidian moonscape rose the summit cone, more than a quarter mile up — tomorrow's project.

It was there that the four tents were placed, sheltered from the wind. Dinner was hot tea, hot soup, and a lot of instant pasta for carbohydrate energy.

The adults went to their bedrolls early, extracting a promise from their teenage charges that this would not be a late night.

"Remember what you did today," said Dr. Oberman, "and what you still have to do tomorrow. Five A.M. wake-up." She slipped into her tent, leaving them in the glow of a single helmet lamp.

"Five A.M., five P.M.," said Bryn wearily. "It's all night here, unless you're talking about high noon."

"Aw, come on," countered Sammi, eyes gleaming. "Think about where we are — up a freak of nature that's halfway to the North Pole, hanging on by our toenails —"

THE CONTEST

"If you say it's extreme," Bryn interrupted, "you're eating the tent."

"Well, it is," Sammi insisted. "We're thumbing our noses at gravity. I love this place! And if you're a real climber, you should, too."

"I'm a climber," Bryn retorted. "I just don't delude myself into thinking this is beautiful. Because even if you could see it, it would still be the armpit of the universe."

"I suppose you're going to dis E, too," Sammi said scornfully.

"It's not *what* you climb; it's that you're *climbing*," Bryn tried to explain. "The physical demands, the personal challenge — "

"Yawn," put in Sammi. "How about you, Dominic? You climb for the rush, right? Or are you searching for your true self like Oprah over here?"

Dominic seemed surprised to be consulted. Then he said slowly, "When I look at something, I automatically try to think of a way to get to the top of it. I don't know why. Maybe because Chris does it. And he got it from my dad. It's like when George Mallory was asked why he was climbing Everest, and he said, 'Because it's there.' "

"He was joking," Perry broke in.

The others looked at him.

"No, really. It was in a book my uncle gave

me. There was a press conference, and one reporter kept asking, 'Why do you want to climb Everest? Why? Why? Why?' And just to shut the guy up, Mallory told him, 'Because it's there.' It was a put-down. It's nothing to base your life on!" He had started off softly, but now he was speaking sharply, his voice full of scorn.

"I read you loud and clear," said Sammi. "You hate this. So why are you here?"

"I made it up that wall, same as you," Perry defended himself.

"Agreed," said Bryn. "You did fine today. But it's pretty obvious to the three of us that you're just not into it. And if we can see it, Cap can see it, too. Why didn't he wash you out?"

"Maybe Cap is a better judge than you guys."

"Or maybe Tilt was right," challenged Sammi, "and your uncle bought you onto this expedition."

Perry smoldered silently in the dim light.

"Is it true?" prompted Bryn.

The flush began in his cheeks, spreading until his many freckles melted together to create a complexion of fire.

"Well, is it?"

And then the dam burst. "You don't know what you're talking about," he said tersely. "My uncle didn't buy me onto this expedition. My uncle bought the whole expedition! He's Joe Sullivan — does that name ring a bell?"

"The founder of Summit Athletic," breathed Dominic, impressed.

"And president, and chairman of the board," Perry finished. "Cap didn't cut me, and I didn't quit for exactly the same reason — because Joe Sullivan always gets what he wants!" He was up, in the tent, and crawling into his sleeping bag before any of them could say a word. As upset as he was, he felt a certain measure of relief that this was finally out in the open. And if the others hated him, then so be it. They'd probably expected something like this anyway. Perry knew that speculation about him had been flying around boot camp. At least that was over.

He snuggled in his bedroll and covered his ears in an attempt not to listen to their conversation. But the quarters were close, and he couldn't help overhearing snippets here and there. Like Bryn's comment: "You know what's really Looney Toons about all this? He's got the guts to take on Everest, but not to tell his uncle that he doesn't want to go."

Or Dominic: "What bugs me is that he's here, and Chris is sitting at home."

"Don't even go there," groaned Sammi.

"Chris had no chance. They needed youth. If Perry wasn't here, ten to one we'd be stuck with Tilt."

Perry was never sure what time he dozed off. But when he awoke, he could hear Dominic's even breathing in the sleeping bag next to him. The glowing face of his watch told him it was after three. He lay there, bone weary, yet wired at the same time.

*Come on, Perry, go back to sleep! Wake-up is less than two hours away.*

Sleep would not come. He tossed and turned for a while, but the air mattress did little to soften the rock floor. His bones, already achy from the climb, began to protest in earnest.

He crept out of the tiny tent, struggling into his jacket and boots as he moved. He stood motionless in the light snow, unwilling to risk even a step in the total darkness. If last night's little episode was repeated up here, he could find himself four thousand feet below, permanently impacted in the glacier. Almost in self-defense, he located the helmet lamp and switched it on.

"Oh." For the first time, he realized he was not alone. Bryn Fiedler stood there facing him. "Couldn't sleep, either?" he asked.

She gave him no answer and began to saunter slowly away.

THE CONTEST

Great, he thought. *Either she just plain hates my guts, or she thinks I'm trying to spy on her trip to the bathroom.*

And then he noticed something peculiar. The girl wore no coat and was bootless.

"Hey, aren't you cold?"

Still no answer, not even any indication that she had heard him. She kept on walking toward — what? There was nothing up here. If you went far enough, you'd just —

"No-o-o-o!"

# CHAPTER SIXTEEN

His heart in his throat, Perry charged across the camp. He grabbed Bryn right at the rim of the shoulder, but she shrugged him off. Her strength and his momentum took the two of them over the edge.

At the last possible second, his fingertips felt rock, and he clamped on in desperation. Sobbing in shock and terror, he tried to scream "Cap!" but no sound came out. All of his life force was channeled into the effort to pull himself back onto the shoulder. It was only a few feet — a single chin-up — but it seemed to take a very long time, and even more effort than the entire day's climb.

And then he found himself lying on level terrain. Bryn was gone. Gone as if she had never been there.

"Cap! Ca-a-ap!"

His cries brought everyone running.

"What's wrong?" roared the team leader.

"She's gone!" Perry howled, beyond hysteria.

"Who?"

THE CONTEST

"Bryn! Bryn! She just walked over the side! She killed herself!"

"Where?"

"Over there!" Still on his hands and knees, Perry led the team to the spot where Bryn had fallen from sight.

Cicero switched on his helmet lamp and shone it into the blackness of the void below. Time ground to a halt in tense agony. If Bryn had plummeted all the way to the glacier, there was no chance that she would be alive.

Here on the southwest face, the ice wall had come away from the rock of the mountain, creating a narrow envelope beginning about thirty feet below them.

There, lying motionless in the bottom of that impossibly thin gap, lay Bryn. The whole party shouted down to her, but she did not respond.

Cicero turned to Perry. "She walked over the side? Just like that?"

"Yeah!"

"That's not it!" Sammi countered, shrill with hysteria. "She was sleepwalking!"

Cicero stared at her. "What?"

"She sleepwalks!" the girl exclaimed. "She did it at boot camp. That's how all the stuff got busted up. It wasn't vandalism. She couldn't help it!"

The team leader was furious. "And you didn't see fit to tell me?"

"And watch a good climber get cut?"

"That girl could be home in bed instead of dead or dying!" snapped Cicero.

The terrible reality crystallized in his gut and radiated outward, freezing his entire body. Sure, he had lost team members before — more than he cared to think about. It was the nature of this dangerous game. But he knew in an instant that this was *different*. Bryn Fiedler was sixteen years old. She should be preparing for the junior prom.

"Bryn!" he roared. "Bryn, can you hear me?"

The form below them was still.

Now Sammi was crying. "She said she'd be okay once the pressure was off! I believed her. I'm so sorry. . . ."

Cap Cicero had no time for tearful apologies. He was a veteran climber in an emergency. Blame was irrelevant now. There were no *should haves*, only *have tos*. Nothing mattered except extricating Bryn from the envelope of ice and, if she was alive, getting her off the mountain and to medical attention.

As panic overtook the others, a calm professionalism descended over him, and he began to bark orders. "Andrea, get on the horn and see when the rangers can get us a helicopter. Lenny, I need crampons, a harness, and some rope."

Perry was wide-eyed as the guides sprang into action. "You're not climbing down there?"

"If you can think of a better way to get her out, I'm all ears."

Sneezy reappeared, his arms laden with gear. As the team leader affixed a top rope to a sturdy boulder, Dr. Oberman returned to the scene, the long-range cell phone at her ear. "They'll give us a chopper, but the pilot won't go close to the mountain until sunup. Around ten o'clock."

"Tell them we'll be waiting," confirmed Cicero, clipping his harness onto the fixed line.

The doctor relayed the information and then called, "They also want to know if we need a medical team for the injured climber."

"I'll let you know in a minute," Cicero replied grimly, and was gone.

Dominic watched in awe as the renowned alpinist rappelled expertly from the top of the shoulder. Cicero covered the distance in a few seconds and stood on the lip. Easing himself into the narrow gap, he began to descend to Bryn.

From above, the others looked on breathlessly. Cicero's lower body disappeared into the opening. But he went no farther.

"Why's he stopping?" asked Sammi.

It was Dr. Oberman who put two and two together. "He's stuck! The gap is too small."

And with that, Dominic was pounding across the shoulder to camp. At the tent, he grabbed his helmet lamp, shrugged into his climbing harness, and strapped on crampons. The sharp points grated jarringly against the naked black rock, but he barely noticed, running as fast as his awkward footwear would allow. There was an unwritten rule of climbing: *The job falls to whoever can get it done.* Right here, right now, thirteen-year-old Dominic Alexis had an advantage that even the great Cap Cicero couldn't match.

"Dominic — come back!" Dr. Oberman cried.

She ran to stop him, but he clipped onto the rope and lowered himself over the side.

Free fall. He swung himself into the cliff face, pushed off with his feet, and dropped some more. The feeling of gravity on his body gave him confidence. The axis of motion was vertical, and Dominic was in his element.

He dropped to the lip to find Cicero chipping at the thick ice with his ax.

He gawked at his youngest team member.

THE CONTEST

"Get out of here, Alexis! I've lost one climber already! No way I'm going to risk a double whammy!"

"I can get down there!" Dominic panted, catching his breath. "I'm smaller than you!"

"Forget it!" roared Cicero. But he examined Dominic's slight frame and mentally pasted it into the narrow passage of uneven ice that stood between Bryn and any chance of rescue. It would take hours to widen the opening with ice tools alone. Bryn — if she was alive at all — would fall victim to shock, hypothermia, frostbite. The only chance was to get her out *fast*.

"All right," he conceded. "But be careful. The last thing I need is two of you trapped down there."

It was like spelunking in an ice cave, only straight down, Dominic reflected. Pressed hard against the rough rock of the mountain's granite core, he squeezed past jagged chunks of ice. The painful, awkward movements were almost comforting to him. It was the style of the Alexis brothers to take the ordinary and turn it vertical. Only this time, there was no Chris to help him, and Bryn's life hung in the balance.

As he descended, the rope that tethered him to Cicero wrapped around his legs. Untangling himself in the unbearably confined space was an arduous task that ate up his two most precious assets — strength and time. Finally, he reached the bottom of the chasm where Bryn lay on her side, battered and bleeding.

The moment of truth: He bent an ear to her slightly open mouth.

THE CONTEST

# CHAPTER SEVENTEEN

Warm breath, faint but regular.

"She's alive!" he howled out.

"How about *you?*" asked Cicero from twenty feet above.

"I'm fine!" Dominic gulped air. "What now?"

The team leader lowered a warm blanket to Dominic, who wrapped it around Bryn's unmoving form. Next, Dominic secured her with three slings — one at her shoulders, one supporting her back, and one at her knees. Cicero tied the tops of these lines onto a single rope dropped from the shoulder above. There, using a rounded rock as a pulley, Dr. Oberman, Sneezy, Sammi, and Perry began to haul her up.

Bryn rose about seven feet before snagging in the jagged ice.

"Stop! Stop!" cried Dominic. "She's stuck! You're crushing her!"

He scrambled up his own rope and tried without success to maneuver Bryn around the protruding chunk of ice. Then he pulled out his ax and began hacking at the obstruction.

EVEREST

"How does it look?" Cicero called down to him.

"Bad." Dominic could hear the panic edging into his voice. "This could take hours."

"We've got hours," he soothed. "Six before the chopper gets here. I'll start cutting a path from the top."

Dominic had been climbing since he was four years old, but this was something he never could have imagined — trapped in the ice on a hostile mountain, chopping away at a two-foot-thick outcropping in a race against the elements and the clock. Each strike of the ax chipped a millimeter or two away. Barely a hair. Dust.

An hour passed. Then two. The repetitive motion of swinging the tool made his shoulder socket throb with pain. He shivered in the forty-below cold as he worked, and ice fragments from Cicero's efforts rained down on him from above.

And then, a voice from a place buried so deep inside him he wasn't even sure it really existed: *Rest.*

"Never!" he seethed, enraged that he would entertain such a thought when Bryn's life was at stake. He began to flail his ax wildly. *Thunk! Thunk! Thunk!* The teeth bit repeatedly into the ice until he realized that the passage was clear and he was exhausting himself for nothing.

THE CONTEST

"Okay!" he rasped, his voice barely audible. Louder: "Okay! Ready to lift!"

Cicero echoed the call, and a moment later, Bryn began to ascend once more. Dominic followed beneath her, kicking his crampons into the ice wall for leverage as he guided his unconscious teammate up through the narrow pathway.

They were getting close. He could see flashes of Cicero's helmet lamp in the thin strip of dark sky above. Then, just a few feet below the lip, Bryn got hung up again. Dominic tried every which way to finesse her around a protruding ice boulder, but it was no use.

The news was grim from above as well.

"I just talked to the ranger station," Dr. Oberman called down to Cicero. "Bad weather on the way!"

Sammi was right beside her. "Well, duh! It hasn't stopped snowing for five seconds since we got here!"

"They grounded the chopper?" Cicero asked in dismay.

"We've got a helicopter window from ten to ten-thirty!" Sneezy supplied. "After that, the high winds come, and we're on our own. The National Weather Service is calling for a foot of snow."

Cicero checked his watch. It was seven-forty. "Take the kids and get down."

Perry was appalled. "But what about Bryn?"

"Don't worry about her," Sneezy said seriously. "She'll be riding in a nice warm chopper while we bust our butts on that wall!"

Sammi was uncertain. "*If* there's a chopper!"

The cameraman grabbed her by the arm and began dragging her back toward camp. "If you're still hanging off that cliff face when the storm hits, you're going to learn the true meaning of extreme!"

That was enough for Perry. "Let's get out of here!"

But Sammi dug in her heels. "What about Dominic?"

On the lip thirty feet below, that was the very subject under discussion. "Kid, there's a storm coming, and I'm sending everybody down," Cicero called down through the ice. "That includes you."

Dominic was horrified. "You're going to *leave* her?"

"I can get her out myself," Cicero assured him. "The chopper's giving us till ten-thirty."

"You won't make it! We've got four feet of ice to cut through!" He swung his ax harder, faster.

"Forget it, Alexis, I'm not risking you!"

"No!" A whirlwind of activity beneath the ice. *Thunk! Thunk!*

THE CONTEST

"You little snot, where do you get off telling me how to run my expedition? I was soloing mountains before you were in diapers!"

*Thunk! Thunk! Thunk!*

The expedition leader's face flamed red. "If you disobey this order, you're *history* on this team! You're not going anywhere with me! Not Everest. Not around the corner to buy a stick of gum. Got it?"

Dominic barely even heard him as he hacked away. His universe, at that moment, was a four-foot mass of ice that had to be cut away in less than three hours. Compared to that, Cap Cicero, SummitQuest, even Dominic's own safety seemed as insignificant as the price of peanuts in Peru.

Cicero was powerless to stop him. He couldn't reach Dominic through the narrow opening in the ice. All he could do was take out his own ax and work at the obstruction from the top. Now the chipping sound had a double rhythm — *thunk-thunk! Thunk-thunk!*

Dr. Oberman lowered the long-range cell phone to Cicero, and the team on the shoulder began the long descent. There was no talk of a summit bid — not with a climber unconscious and a blizzard on the way. The video camera remained in Sneezy's pack. This was one part of

SummitQuest that the general public would never see.

Dominic had no watch. He measured the hours by the burning fire in his arm and the numbing cold that gripped the rest of his body. His fatigue went far beyond what he had felt after ascending the four-thousand-foot wall. This was a single motion — the swing of an ice tool — repeated without rest for countless hours. Doubt and dread plagued him. Was he tiring to the point where he'd have no strength left to get *himself* out of this frozen tomb? And even if he could make it back to the shoulder, would he have the energy and the will to front-point nearly a vertical mile down to the glacier?

*Doesn't matter. Not important. Keep working. Don't stop.*

He was aware of a brightening in the sky. Sunrise, or the closest thing to it in the permanent gloomy overcast. The sound came soon after the light, low but audible, even from under the ice. Almost like a slow-motion drumroll.

A helicopter!

THE CONTEST

# CHAPTER EIGHTEEN

*"Ten o'clock!"* Cicero bellowed the time check.

Dominic sized up the foot-thick obstruction that still imprisoned Bryn and took it apart mentally blow by blow. They had half an hour. Would there be enough time?

*There has to be!*

Brandishing the ax with both hands, he hacked with an unbridled ferocity that surprised even him. He could hear Cicero begging him to calm down, to budget his energy, but Dominic knew that right now fever pitch was the only speed for him. He didn't dare slacken the pace for even a second for fear that his whole body would shut down.

*Thunk! Thunk!*

"Ten-fifteen!"

It seemed to go on forever. Hours — no, they didn't have hours. But minutes felt like hours in this endless motion, endless exhaustion, endless ice. The edges of his vision began to blur.

*Don't faint on me now!*

EVEREST

"Ten-twenty-five!"

*Thunk! Thunk!*

Above him, Cicero was barking into the phone, "Give us five more minutes! *Two more minutes!*"

*Thunk! Thunk!*

And then: "Heads up!"

Cicero's boot broke through the obstruction, raining ice and snow down on Dominic's head. Marshaling every ounce of strength he had left, the boy dug in his crampons and put his full weight under Bryn in an attempt to push her up to Cicero. The team leader grabbed the injured climber and hauled her onto the lip. "Now!" he bawled into the phone.

Barely conscious, Dominic crawled out of the envelope after being entombed for seven hours. Wobbling on unsteady feet beside Cicero, he noted that the weather had already changed. Howling wind blew snow in their faces. Surely, the full force of the storm could not be far behind.

When the helicopter became visible, it was a lot closer than Dominic expected. It seemed to explode out of the gray-white squall sixty feet in front of them, coming up fast.

"He's too low!" shouted Dominic.

At the last minute, the pilot veered off, looping

THE CONTEST

up and away from the mountain, vanishing once more. When the chopper reappeared, it was higher, descending gradually toward them.

Cicero put an iron grip on Dominic's shoulders and eased him to his knees to keep him clear of the spinning rotor blades. There wasn't enough room to land on the lip, so the pilot set the nose wheel down on the rim of ice and hovered — a difficult and treacherous piece of flying. The helicopter was "parked," but it couldn't stay that way forever.

Cicero climbed into the chopper, grabbed Bryn under the arms, and hauled her aboard. Then he reached out a hand to Dominic.

A powerful gust of wind buffeted the mountain, plastering Dominic against the rock face. The nose wheel slipped off the lip, and the helicopter seemed to bounce in the air, the deadly rotors dipping toward him.

"*Duck!*" howled Cicero.

With no time to think or even breathe, Dominic dove back into the opening.

The lethal blades shaved the ice at the top of the lip before the pilot yanked on the control and drew the chopper up and away from the mountain.

Falling. Dominic kicked out with both legs. Crampon points dug into the walls and he lurched to a stop. Hand over hand, he climbed back into the wind and snow. A desperate scan of his surroundings. The helicopter was gone.

"Cap!"

No answer. The panic began in his stomach, leaping up the back of his throat. All their lines, bolts, and ice screws had descended with the rest of the team. Could he make it down that wall of ice, alone, unroped, through a howling blizzard?

*Chris should be here. He's the better climber. He'd find a way out of this.*

He reached inside his jacket and clutched at his brother's vial of Dead Sea sand, which was never going to Everest. Which might not even make it off Lucifer's Claw . . .

"*Dominic!!*"

The cry was so faint that he would have missed it if not for the frantic urgency in the voice. With a roar of machinery, the helicopter burst out of the driving gray snow. Cicero crouched at the hatch, dangling a rope that blew every which way.

A screaming fight was in progress between the team leader and the pilot. How close to Dominic did they dare go?

"If the wind currents blow us into the mountain, then none of us make it home!" the pilot argued.

"That's a thirteen-year-old kid out there!" Cicero shouted back. "If you land this bird without him, you're gonna *wish* you'd crashed into a mountain!"

*I'm lost*, Dominic thought to himself. *They can't get close enough. Not in this wind.*

No sooner had the idea crossed his mind than the wind died and there was a moment of sudden, unexpected calm. All at once, the snow was falling directly downward, and the rope hung straight and unmoving from the chopper.

"Get him! *Get him!*" roared Cicero.

Slow motion — that's how it seemed to Dominic. Waiting for the helicopter to approach was the longest few seconds of his life. Thirty feet away . . . then twenty . . . then ten . . .

As he unclipped his harness from the rope, he was struck by a flash of foresight. There was no explanation for it. Call it climber's instinct. He just *knew*.

*The wind's coming back.*

Dominic Alexis took two powerful steps and hurled himself into the thin air — a spectacular dyno more than a mile above the Atkinson Glacier.

"No-o-o!" cried Cicero in horror.

And there, in midleap, Dominic found a strange serenity. He wasn't in Alaska at all. In his mind he was in the valley outside the Summit complex in Colorado, making the jump that would solve the Mushroom. It was madness to spring off a mountain, but no climber could resist the move that would unravel a tough problem.

He felt the jolt of the returning wind in the small of his back, driving him onward. When his mitts first touched the rope, he was startled for a moment, as if he hadn't expected to make it. Then he grabbed on for dear life and hung there as the team leader hauled him aboard.

Cap Cicero, veteran of a hundred expeditions and every tragedy and rescue in the book, threw his arms around his youngest climber and squeezed until Dominic could barely breathe. "I thought we lost you, kid!" he panted again and again. "I thought we lost you!"

"I'm right here, Cap," Dominic managed. "I'm fine."

The pilot pulled back on the controls, and the chopper swung away from Lucifer's Claw. "Let's get out of here," he said, his face white. "We've already used up eight of our nine lives."

THE CONTEST

# CHAPTER NINETEEN

Bryn Fiedler suffered a broken arm and ankle, four cracked ribs, and a severe concussion. She also had mild frostbite on her fingers and toes, but the doctors said she would make a full recovery.

"Doctors in Alaska see a lot of frostbite," Cicero informed her. "So they know what they're talking about."

Sammi, Perry, and Dominic visited her the next day in the hospital in Juneau. She was propped up in bed, her arm in a cast, bandages on her head, hands, and feet.

She started when she saw them. "Oh, it's you guys. I thought you were my parents."

"They're coming up from Chicago?" asked Sammi.

She nodded. "Separate planes, separate rent-a-cars. I guess that's how things are going to be in my family from now on — separate." She shifted in bed to face Dominic. "Cap told me how you saved my life."

"Anybody would have done it," Dominic mumbled uncomfortably.

"No," she said seriously. "If Cap had chosen

your brother instead of you like everybody thought, I'd be dead right now. Do you honestly think Chris could have made it into that tiny chasm to get me out? He's almost as big as Cap." She regarded the slight boy, shamefaced. "I'm sorry I didn't have more faith in you. You deserve to go to Everest."

"I don't think anybody's going to E anymore," Sammi put in sadly. "Cap's on the phone with Tony Devlin right now. Word is they're going to scrap the expedition."

All eyes turned to Perry.

"What's everybody looking at me for? You think my uncle calls to ask how to run Summit?" He added, "But my guess is they'll cancel."

"You're relieved," Bryn accused.

"You bet I am," Perry said feelingly. "If all this stuff could happen on Lucifer's Claw, how could we go up three times as high?"

"It's my fault," Bryn mourned. "I thought my sleepwalking would stop when we got out of boot camp. And now I'm lucky to be alive." She sighed. "I ruined it for everybody."

Sammi put a hand on her shoulder. "I guess this means cliff jumping is back in the plan. Caleb will be happy."

And then, a gruff but familiar voice: "Caleb is out of luck."

THE CONTEST

Cap Cicero strode into the room. "I just got off the phone with Tony Devlin. SummitQuest is still on!"

Perry was wide-eyed. "But what about yesterday?"

"If you kids can get out of a jam like that, then you're *ready* for Everest," the team leader said positively. "Even you, Noonan. You held it together up there."

Perry didn't know whether to be horrified or flattered.

"But not me, right?" Dominic ventured sadly.

"What are you talking about?" asked Bryn.

"I disobeyed a direct order," Dominic explained, "and Cap washed me out."

Cicero put an arm around his narrow shoulders. "Kid, after what I saw yesterday, I'm amazed I ever climbed anything *without* you. Yeah, you wouldn't listen, and I was mad. But we saved a team member because of it, and that trumps everything." His smile vanished as suddenly as it had appeared. "So no cheeseburgers when you get home — you're in training! We leave for Nepal in three weeks."

"*I'll* have a cheeseburger for you," Bryn volunteered wanly. "It's the least I can do."

"One more thing," Cicero added. "Nobody talks to the press about what happened, got it?

That comes straight from the Summit board. If a reporter asks why Bryn isn't going, just say she turned an ankle on the test climb."

"I didn't turn it; I *broke* it," Bryn reminded him. "Along with every other bone in my body."

"You broke it because you turned it," the expedition leader explained glibly.

"Yeah," Perry winced at the mere memory, "at the bottom of a fifty-foot fall."

"What about her replacement?" asked Sammi. "Who's going to be the fourth team member?"

Dominic snapped to eager attention. "It's my brother, right? We're taking Chris?"

Cicero shook his head sadly. "I'm afraid not."

THE CONTEST

# EPILOGUE

**E-mail message**
**To: BU@national-daily.com**
**Subject: SummitQuest**

Good news! Summit made Cap put me back on the team. At least somebody knows a real climber when they see one.

We leave for Nepal on March 15. Now I can continue to E-mail your newspaper more dirt about the SummitQuest boneheads. Don't worry, Cap doesn't suspect a thing. He still thinks it's sour grapes from some loser who washed out.

**Tilt Crowley**

P.S. Remember, when I summit Everest, I'm doubling my usual fee. The next time you see me, I'll be a star!

EVEREST

# Another great trilogy from
# Gordon Korman

and look for even more Island excitement online!
## Visit
# www.scholastic.com/island

- ■ BFW 0-439-16456-7 **Island#1: Shipwreck** **$4.50 US**
- ■ BFW 0-439-16457-5 **Island#2: Survival** **$4.50 US**
- ■ BFW 0-439-16452-4 **Island#3: Escape** **$4.50 US**

**Available wherever you buy books, or use this order form.**

**Scholastic Inc., P.O. Box 7502, Jefferson City, MO 65102**

Please send me the books I have checked above. I am enclosing $_____ (please add $2.00 to cover shipping and handling). Send check or money order—no cash or C.O.D.s please.

Name_____ Birth date_____

Address_____

City_____ State/Zip_____

Please allow four to six weeks for delivery. Offer good in U.S.A. only. Sorry, mail orders are not available to residents of Canada. Prices subject to change.

■▲ SCHOLASTIC

IL802